OLIVER & Mia

OLIVER & Mia

Lovingly written by

By

Riano D. McFarland

Copyright © 2022 by Riano D. McFarland.

Amazon Control Numbers

ISBN-13 Hardcover: ISBN: 9798846766068
Softcover: ISBN: 9798846756779
eBook ASIN: B0BB743G51

All rights reserved. No part of this book may be reproduced or transmitted in any form or by any means, electronic or mechanical, including photocopying, recording, or by an information storage and retrieval system, without permission in writing from the copyright owner.

This is a work of fiction. names, characters, places, and incidents either are the product of the author's imagination or are used fictitiously, and any resemblance to any actual person, living or dead, events, or locales is entirely coincidental.

Any figures depicted in stock imagery are models, and such images are being used for illustrative purposes only.

For information regarding other novels by Riano D. McFarland, please contact:

> www.vanityinconline.com/BOOKS.htm or
> vanityinc@cox.net

DEDICATION

This novel is dedicated to those who understand and enjoy the power of the written word. There is nothing quite like the feeling of being immersed in a book and losing oneself in its pages.

Centuries from now, when we are but fading memories, our culture, our achievements, and also our depictions of the world in which we now live, will be studied based on what we've left behind for the next great civilization to explore. On that day, I pray that they will gravitate towards the inspirational and the good, and therein, find my stories.

CHAPTER 1

IF A WISE man were fortunate enough to survive a gunfight in Virginia City, Nevada, during the height of the gold and silver rush in the 1870s, he would take that as a sign to pack up and move on before the kinfolk of his adversary came looking for him. Unfortunately, there weren't many wise men who could simply call it quits after mining enough precious metal to provide for the next five generations of their descendants.

No matter how much wealth they'd accumulated, the allure of silver and gold was like a grappling hook for most people mining or panning for it. There was never enough, and the temptation of going back for one final load had proven to be the disastrous end for many a wealthy yet greedy prospector.

So often, that person lying face-down in the road, bleeding out into an uncaring patch of dirt audacious enough to call itself Main Street, would soon be followed to boot hill by the lucky fool whose carefully measured 45-caliber chunk of lead had dropped him there.

Being undone and relieved of a sack of precious metal after being shot through the heart by that metal's most un-precious ugly cousin was the ultimate irony. Nevertheless, trading lead for silver and gold was a common and lucrative endeavor in the North American West during the late 1800s, with the victors of such confrontations often being discovered face-down behind the nearest saloon after purchasing a celebratory round of drinks for the cheering patrons at the bar.

There were innumerable unknown faces in western cities and towns, which popped up overnight and disappeared just as quickly. Many of them were referred to as "strangers," and if they were smart, they stuck with that handle until they had safely returned with their bounties to their homes back east.

Of course, there were those who fancied themselves as celebrities in their own minds, seeking glorified recognition for having been a fraction of a second faster than their opponents on one occasion or another. In addition to gunslingers like Billy the Kid, Butch Cassidy, John Wesley Hardin, and Clay Allison, there were countless others whose winning sprees culminated in one or two, before they also ended up face down on Main Street, with their pockets several golden ounces lighter.

Names like The Rattlesnake Kid, Lightning Luke Cain, and Dead Eye William Dodd were mere flashes in the pan in the annals of history, claiming the title of "Fastest Gun in the West" for as little as a week to as long as six months before being usurped. In the end, it was the speed of their tongues rather than the quickness of their draws that undid each of them.

During the beginning of the California gold rush, prospectors would commonly share the details of their daily haul in pseudo-friendly competition with one another. That quickly changed when new arrivals, hoping to cash in on Mother Nature's hidden treasures, discovered that the most generous stakes had already been claimed, and the pitiful glitter yielded by panning the remaining streams and waterways was barely enough to pay for their daily bread.

With the frustration of realizing they'd crossed the entire continent for a mere pittance of the wealth in the pockets of other prospectors came the inevitable result of shattered dreams: desperation. Soon, those desperate men, realizing they'd traveled nearly three thousand miles to wind up penniless and unable to return to their previous lives, took desperate measures, giving birth to the legend of the Wild West.

Despite the rampant lawlessness surrounding them, there were those who could resist the temptation of the siren songs of gold and silver. They came near the beginning of the rush and with a clearly defined objective. Upon reaching that objective, they cashed in their treasures, took their money, and returned to their families and their lives in cities like New York, Boston, Chicago, and Saint Louis. There, they could finance businesses, invest in lucrative innovative opportunities, or simply live out the remainder of their lives in peace and comfort.

For five years, one unremarkable stranger had kept to himself. He worked hard and in isolation after staking a bountiful claim that produced copious amounts of silver and gold. He'd never bragged or disclosed the location of his mining bonanza, nor frequented Virginia City, until he was ready to cash out and go home.

Due to the boom resulting from ongoing mining operations associated with the Comstock Lode, Virginia City, Nevada, was flush with cash and able to purchase his substantial booty. The looks on the faces of the agents at the Virginia City Gold and Silver Exchange were a testament to the rarity of such a transaction being conducted by a sole individual. Unlike the company men who showed up each afternoon, surrounded by a posse of armed guards, this ordinary-looking stranger arrived first thing in the morning, on a wagon drawn by two mules, and left with nearly five hundred thousand dollars! Ten minutes later, most of that money was under the protection of Western Union agents, who handed the stranger a receipt for his wire-transfer into an account in Boston, Massachusetts.

For his eastbound journey, he kept a pouch of gold ore and a thousand dollars in cash. However, there was nothing about him that would indicate either of those things were in his possession. It was still early, and before getting underway, he decided to have breakfast in a small restaurant across the street from the Western Union office.

When he entered through the open front door, the handful of people inside gave him only a cursory glance before turning back to a frightened little girl sitting at a table in the far corner. Taking a seat on the opposite side of the restaurant, he stared out the window, telling himself, *"It's none of my business."*

A few seconds later, a smiling woman approached with a large cup and a pot of hot coffee, asking, "Just coffee, or would you like to try some breakfast this morning? The biscuits just came out of the oven, and I'd be happy to get you a ham steak and some scrambled eggs to go with them. "

"That sounds perfect," said the man, nodding and smiling politely.

"Well, my name is Louann, and I'll be right back," said the delightful woman before turning and heading back towards the kitchen.

As he sat there sipping the aromatic coffee, the smell of the biscuits lingered tantalizingly in the air. It had been over a year since he'd eaten a sit-down meal, and his mouth was already watering at the thought of it.

"Well, what are we supposed to do, Sheriff Walsh? We run a restaurant here, not an orphanage," said the short, stocky woman while wiping her flour-covered hands on her apron. "I'm sorry to hear about her parents and all, but this ain't no place to raise a child."

"Nancy, it would only be until we could reach someone from her family in Boston," said the sheriff. "I'm sure they'll send someone to collect her, so you'll only need to take care of her for a few weeks at most."

"But, what if they don't come for her? Even worse, what if there's no one there who *can* come for her?" Nancy protested. "This place keeps us hopping all the time, and our hands are already full, so as much as I'd like to help you, I'm not willing to assume the responsibility of raising an orphaned child."

"Here you go," said the young woman, placing the plate of ham, eggs, and biscuits in front of the hungry stranger and asking, "Would you like some peach preserves or molasses to go with your biscuits?"

"Peach preserves would be nice," he answered. As the server turned back towards the kitchen, the stranger said, "Hey, I don't mean to be nosey, but can you tell me what happened to the girl over there? From what I overheard; it sounds pretty bad. "

Lowering her voice to a whisper, Louann said, "Well, her name is Mia, and she walked into town this morning. Someone found her and took her over to the sheriff's office. Apparently, her parents were robbed and murdered yesterday, and she walked all night to get here. "

As two additional diners entered the restaurant, the woman said, "I'll be right back with your preserves," before nodding at the two newcomers and heading into the kitchen again.

"Can I at least leave her here while I send a telegraph to Boston and try to locate her family there?" asked Sheriff Walsh. "Nancy, you know I wouldn't ask if I had any other options, but you're the only one I can turn to at the moment."

Looking disdainfully at the young girl, Nancy said, "You have two days, and after that, if you don't come for her, I'll toss her out like dirty bathwater. There ain't no such thing as a free ride here, and I ain't about to make an exception for some child who I don't even know."

As he sat there quietly eating his breakfast, the stranger noticed that the young girl wasn't even paying attention to the conversation between Nancy and Sheriff Walsh. Instead, a look of abject fear was plastered across her face as she stared mutely at the two men who'd just entered the restaurant. Not only had she recognized them, but they had also recognized her, and when Sheriff Walsh left the establishment, the two men visibly relaxed, as if relieved to have thus far gone undetected.

"It's none of my business," he said to himself as he attempted to focus on the delicious breakfast before him, to no avail.

A few seconds later, Louann rushed past, placing a small bowl of peach preserves on his table before hurrying over to the two dubious gentlemen, now seated between him and the recently orphaned child. All he wanted was to finish his breakfast, settle his tab, and get the hell out of Virginia City.

After five years of sticking to his meticulously developed plan, he was determined to see it through without being side-tracked. Accordingly, he finished his coffee, wolfed down the rest of his breakfast, and left a very generous half-dollar on the table to cover his meal. A few minutes later, he was leaving Virginia City, en route to Reno, where he would sell the mules and the wagon before boarding a train for the Atlantic Coast. With a bit of luck, he'd be back in Boston within a week.

He'd gone nearly four miles before his conscience erected an insurmountable obstacle in his path. It didn't take a seasoned officer of the law to see what was going on in that restaurant. Those two men had either killed that child's parents, or they'd been there when it happened. Clearly, they were looking for an opportunity to eliminate the last remaining witness who could tie them to the murder.

Sheriff Walsh was either too overwhelmed or too preoccupied with other murders to dive headlong into another investigation, and the stranger had his doubts as to whether the sheriff could locate the child's relatives, if he even bothered to try.

When he walked back into the restaurant, the two men were standing across from Nancy, trying to convince her to turn the girl over to them. Although she wasn't very keen on the idea of adopting the orphaned child, it was obvious to her that relinquishing custody of Mia to these two dubious characters would end catastrophically.

"Just hand her over, and we'll be on our way," said the taller of the two gentlemen. "No one will be the wiser, and you can simply wash your hands of the whole ordeal."

Nancy was a stern but godly woman, and when the would-be kidnapper invoked Pontius Pilate, inferring that she could simply betray the little girl by washing her hands of the entire ordeal, they'd lost any chance of peacefully removing her from the establishment.

Just as one of the gunmen rested his hand on the butt of his Colt.45 Peacemaker, a voice from behind him said, "Mia?"

This time, every head in the now-crowded restaurant turned to look, as the stranger said, "Mia honey, I heard what happened, and I'm here to take you back to Boston."

Mia instinctively knew she could trust this tall, mysterious stranger with kind eyes, and she said, "Uncle Peter! You came for me!" All eyes were upon them as Mia rushed over and wrapped her arms around the strange man, saying, "I knew you would be here!"

Since his westward journey began, he'd been as inconspicuous as a rainworm. Every eye in the room of this restaurant, bustling with activity, was trained squarely on the two of them.

"How about we go over to Sheriff Walsh's office and tell him I'll be escorting you back to Boston?" suggested the man who had suddenly become Uncle Peter. Taking Mia's hand in his, he led her out the front door and diagonally across the street to the jailhouse.

The sheriff was legitimately surprised to see the two of them entering the building, and was all too eager to accept this as a solution, despite the absolute incredulity of it. After having "Uncle Peter" sign an impromptu custody document, Sheriff Walsh released Mia into his care with no further questions asked. Honestly, he was glad at least one problem had been taken off his plate for the day.

After helping Mia up onto the hard wooden bench seat of the wagon, he turned to find one of the men from the restaurant standing a few yards away from him with his hand hovering menacingly over the pearl-handled grip of his pistol.

"Do you know who I am?" asked the man.

"Does it matter?" countered the stranger, nonchalantly.

"Around these parts, people call me Blink Masterson," boasted the cocky young gunslinger looking to add another notch to his reputation.

"Well, I'm from around these parts, and I've never heard of you," answered the stranger, squaring up with Blink Masterson, as the two men moved slowly toward the center of the street.

"Well, what should we put on your headstone, because your name sure as hell ain't Uncle Pete?" Blink snarled.

"Here's the thing," said the stranger. "If you hear me say my name, you're already dead."

The next instant, Blink Masterson's body flinched almost imperceptibly as he reached for the holstered colt strapped to his thigh. Suddenly, he was staring into the sun before a dark figure knelt over him, blotting it out completely and coming to within inches of his face.

"Oliver," whispered the stranger, staring deeply into eyes that slowly glazed over before dilating completely.

CHAPTER 2

OLIVER BLACKSTONE WAS a former United States marshal in the great state of Texas. For more than a decade, he'd hunted the worst of the worst fugitives; rudderless men guided only by their own greed and self-serving interests.

They were thieves and murderers who grazed the land in search of easy marks. Without an ounce of remorse, they would rob and kill an entire family for a few ounces of gold, then burn through the loot in a fraction of the time it took for that hard-working family to earn it. Once it was gone, there were plenty of other naïve travelers just waiting to be relieved of their precious life savings.

Marshal Blackstone was a relentless hunter of such ruthless men. He'd stalk them like a wolf, crisscrossing Texas, New Mexico, and the surrounding Indian and Mexican territories, rounding up and bringing lawless men to justice. Every single one of them believed that they would be the gunman who finally ended his merciless crusade to round them all up. None of them ever succeeded.

After ten years and more than two dozen fugitives crossed off of the US Marshals Service's "Most Wanted" list, only a handful of those fugitives lived long enough to feel the hangman's noose around their necks. Most of them died where they stood, shortly after hearing the words, "I'm Marshal Oliver Blackstone, and I'm here to take you in, dead or alive."

For the United States Marshals Service, he was an invaluable asset. For the killers attempting to escape justice, he was the Grim Reaper.

Due to the sheer number of murderers whose rampages he'd abruptly terminated, the unethical criminals remaining on his to-do list decided to reverse the hunt by placing a one-hundred-thousand-dollar bounty on his head. Having beaten the odds so often, Marshal Blackstone decided it was time to quit the game and leave Texas, opting to relocate to the Eastern United States, where he could simply assimilate into the more densely populated region of New England.

Since his withdrawal from the US Marshals Service had been mandated by his superiors, he would continue to receive his monthly salary indefinitely and remain a credentialed US marshal, despite not being required to work.

That would have been the closing chapter of his legacy had it not been for a teacher; an elementary school teacher named Sarah Hutchins, to be more precise. She was everything the criminals he'd hunted for a third of his life were not. She was kind, nurturing, intelligent, and, oh sweet Jesus, was she pretty!

Suddenly, Oliver realized why men were willing to risk everything by heading west in search of treasure upon which to build a future for a family. As a marshal, he'd had no roots and no reason to wish for more than his monthly paycheck and the pro-rated bounty he collected for the outlaws he brought in, covered in a bedroll, and draped across the back of a tired horse.

He'd put some of that money aside; however, in his mind, it wasn't nearly enough to provide the comfortable life he felt Sarah deserved, and that he was determined to provide for her. Her father had built his fortune operating a steel mill in Boston and would certainly not have been impressed with Oliver's rather humble savings.

For Sarah, none of that mattered. The day he smiled at her while holding the door open for her at the bank, Sarah's insides turned to jelly, and despite the haughty manner in which she conducted herself, she became completely infatuated with him.

From that day forward, she went to the bank at exactly the same time each Friday, whether she needed to or not. To her delight, that seemed to mesh perfectly with this handsome stranger's own weekly visits, and after what seemed an eternity, he finally introduced himself as Oliver Blackstone.

To his great surprise, she eagerly accepted his invitation to join him for a picnic in a park near the elementary school where she worked. Following that day, their Saturday afternoon picnics became a regular affair, and after an extended courtship, Oliver asked Sarah's father, Leonard Hutchins, for his daughter's hand in marriage. His reply was an immediate and emphatic "No!"

Leonard Hutchins was unwilling to condone the marriage of his only daughter to a man with no obvious means of supporting her. With numerous suitors from Boston's high society vying for her affections, Leonard Hutchins hoped Sarah would eventually come to her senses and opt for a life of comfort and a secure future with one of them.

Unfortunately, none of them had Oliver's hazel eyes or chiseled jawline, and the worldly manner in which he carried himself was unique to him and impossible to replicate. When he asked if she would give him five years to build a proper financial foundation that even her father couldn't deny, she hesitantly agreed, saying,

"Oliver, you are the man who holds my heart in your hands. I would wait a lifetime for you. "

After revealing his plan to Sarah, and assuring her that he would stick to it without deviation, he left Boston with a sense of motivation he would not have believed possible. He purchased a parcel of land in the New England countryside and made regular monthly mortgage payments until he'd paid it off completely, only three years later.

The entire time, he sent Sarah weekly telegraphs without fail, advising her of his progress but never revealing the volume of wealth he had amassed for their future together. Far too often, careless men had been betrayed by the very operators transmitting their dispatches, and experience had taught Oliver to avoid such problems by treating all of them as potential criminal informants.

Furthermore, he never used the same telegraph office for consecutive transmissions. Instead, he would alternate between cities just in case his actions were being circumspectly monitored. After five years, his efforts at maintaining anonymity had been successful, and with over a half-million dollars' worth of silver and gold in his war chest, it was time to return to Boston and his beloved Sarah.

The gunfight right outside the sheriff's office had caused an unforeseen delay in his departure, and in order to expedite things, he confidentially informed Sheriff Walsh that he was a credentialed United States Marshal, and after a brief inquiry with the Virginia City field office, those credentials were confirmed. Furthermore, the field office notified the sheriff of the bounty on Blink Masterson and directed him to pay out the rightful bounty to Marshal Blackstone.

Following five years of relative invisibility, more information regarding his true identity had been revealed during the past hour than had otherwise been since his arrival in the northwestern territory. It was the kind of information that evil men would seize upon in hopes of claiming that hundred-thousand-dollar bounty, still in circulation.

Had he been traveling alone as nothing more than an anonymous drifter, regaining and keeping a relatively low profile would have been remarkably simple. However, following a very public gunfight and his assumption of responsibility for a seven-year-old Mia Hampton, who, coincidentally, had been the sole eyewitness to the murder of her parents, Oliver's journey from Virginia City, Nevada, to Boston, Massachusetts, would now be anything but uneventful.

He'd performed secure witness transport operations numerous times and was well aware of the dangers they entailed. Based on the meager size of the bounty for Blink Masterson, it was obvious that he was not the one in charge. Most likely, he'd been dispatched to clean up the loose ends of a poorly executed robbery, and the moment his gang leader discovered that he was dead and who had killed him, the Devil's floodgates would open, and the hounds of Hell would be coming for both him and Mia.

Just a few hours earlier, he'd left Virginia City behind, with nothing but clear blue skies ahead of him. With over a half-million dollars in his private bank account, he'd planted the seeds of generational wealth, even without the financial backing of Leonard Hutchins. While traveling alone, he would have been more than capable of ushering anyone coming between him and his darling Sarah into the afterlife in only the blink of an eye.

For whatever reason, fate had guided him into that restaurant where an innocent child, who'd just endured the brutal murder of her parents, was desperately in need of an angel. It could not have been a coincidence. Oliver did not believe in coincidence.

Upon leaving town the first time, after only four miles, he'd encountered a large female grey wolf in the middle of the trail, standing over a dead coyote at the crest of a hill. The wolf did not move, and when Oliver stopped the wagon a few yards away, their gazes met, and they stared into each other's eyes for several seconds before two small cubs peeked curiously out from behind her. Slowly, the wolf turned and ushered her babies over the hill and down the other side, where they disappeared from view.

The significance of that encounter was not lost on Oliver. That mama wolf had been faced with a similar choice: protect her cubs with her life, or leave them to the mercy of the coyote. The wolf had chosen correctly. Now, Oliver must choose correctly too.

Fortunately, he'd arrived just in time to correct his original oversight, and now it was up to him to get them safely back to Boston.

Once they reached the relative security of the train departing from Reno, Nevada, the remainder of their cross-country journey would be manageable. However, between Virginia City and Reno, there were twenty-seven miles of often rough terrain to cover, and every single outlaw west of Texas would have a hundred thousand reasons to kill them both.

CHAPTER 3

BY THE TIME the witness statements were taken, Oliver was cleared, and the bounty for Blink Masterson had been settled, it was much too late in the day to depart Virginia City with a child in tow. Although Mia had proven to be remarkably quick-witted for a seven-year-old, there were now factors to be considered which would certainly threaten both their safety, especially when travelling after sunset.

In a mule-drawn wagon, they would need a full day to reach Reno, and with everyone in town talking about the stranger who'd outdrawn Blink Masterson, the last place Oliver wanted to be, was alone in the wilderness with Mia. At least in Virginia City, they would have the benefit of safety in numbers, discouraging both animal and human predators from viewing them as easy prey. On the other hand, being stationary for the next sixteen hours would give every gunslinger in the region ample time to reach Virginia City and challenge the unknown wildcard who had just been vaulted to the top of "the list."

In Oliver's experience, the last place any sober-minded individual wanted to find themselves was on "the list." It was an unofficial ranking kept only in the minds of those hoping to be at the top of it, and no matter where you ranked, everyone below but within striking distance of that mark immediately set their sights on taking you down. In and around a boom-town like Virginia City, there could be a dozen or more gunmen patiently awaiting such an opportunity. For Oliver, it wasn't even a question of *if* they would come, but rather... *when.*

Although Sheriff Walsh didn't publicly reveal the disbursement of the bounty funds to Oliver, he didn't really need to. The slippery-tongued agent at the Western Union office, whether intentionally or unintentionally, revealed the fact that Oliver had wired nearly a half-million dollars into his private account earlier that day, casually declaring, "He's probably one of the richest men in Virginia City, and now he's collecting bounty money on top of that! It must be nice," he muttered while counting out the twenty-five hundred dollars in large bills and sliding them across the counter to the sheriff.

After leaving the sheriff's office, Oliver and Mia made a bee-line for the International Hotel. When they crossed the empty lobby and approached the reception desk, the smiling gentleman behind it asked, "How may I help you, sir?"

"I'd like to book a room for the young lady, and I have some items I'd like to store in the hotel vault until morning," Oliver replied.

Curiously raising an eyebrow, the man asked, "Are you a frequent guest?"

It was a question Oliver had actually expected. During the course of their official duties, United States marshals often used the International Hotel while conducting investigations and regularly stored sensitive materials in the hotel's secure vault.

"Actually, I won't be staying the night, so you may enter her name, Mia Hampton, in the guest register," Oliver explained. Placing a five-dollar bill on the counter, he said, "This should cover the room, along with dinner tonight and breakfast tomorrow morning, and please make sure her meals are served inside the room."

After logging Mia into the hotel register, the prim gentleman handed Oliver the key to a room on the first floor. Placing it on the counter, Oliver slid it back to him, saying, "I'd prefer a room at the far end of the third floor please."

Following a moment of hesitation, the man produced another key, and Oliver escorted Mia up to her room on the third floor. After inspecting everything thoroughly, he sat next to her on the bed, saying, "I know you've been through a lot during the past couple of days, and I am so very sorry about what happened to your mom and dad." Taking her hand in his, he said, "You've been through more than any little girl should ever have to face, but I promise you, I'm going to get you back to your family in Boston, all right."

Mia nodded wordlessly, and Oliver stood and walked towards the door.

"I'm not a little girl; I'm almost eight," said Mia, stopping Oliver in his tracks.

Smiling, he turned to look back at her, saying, "Really? Almost eight? Oh my," he replied. "You're already a young lady." Tipping his hat, he said, "I'm sorry, and I apologize for the oversight, ma'am."

"It's okay," said Mia.

By the look on her face, Oliver could tell that there was something on her mind, and he asked, "Is there anything else?"

"I was just wondering," she said, obviously feeling somewhat uncomfortable.

"Wondering about what?" asked Oliver, curiously.

"Well, I know you're not my uncle Peter, because he's back in Boston," she said, hesitantly. "But... I don't know what to call you."

Oliver could already see tears forming in her eyes as she struggled to find the right words.

Finally, in a shaky, hesitant voice, she asked, "If you tell me your name, are you going to kill me too?" before completely breaking down in tears.

Oliver's eyes involuntarily flew wide open, and he rushed over to her, kneeling on the floor beside the bed, saying, "No no no, Mia," while wrapping his arms around her. He could feel her sobbing into his shirt as he held her protectively against him and softly said, "I will never, ever hurt you princess, and I promise you... neither will anyone else."

After a moment, her sobs ebbed, and he slowly pulled away from her. "You can call me Oliver," he said, gently brushing the tears from her cheeks.

Mia nodded, and Oliver noticed that, for the first time since meeting her, she was smiling.

Once again, Oliver rose to his feet and headed to the door, opening it, and saying, "Goodnight, Mia."

"Goodnight, Oliver," she replied, as he slipped out the door, closing and securing it behind him.

Upon returning to the front desk, Oliver approached the attentive receptionist again. Looking sternly into the man's eyes, he said, "Other than the three of us, no one knows she's staying here, and I trust that will remain the case."

"Of course... Officer?" stated the man, inquisitively attempting to confirm Oliver's law-enforcement credentials without asking him for them directly.

Ignoring the insinuated question, Oliver said, "I'll be back in the morning," while reaching inside his shirt and removing a medium-sized leather purse branded with the official insignia of the United States Marshals Service. Placing it on the countertop and sliding it across to the hospitality agent, he said, "If you'd be so kind and store this in your vault, I'll be here at 7:00 a.m. sharp to collect both of them."

"As you wish, sir," said the man, nodding and adding, "Have a pleasant evening."

With Mia now settled safely into her room, Oliver left the hotel and went to the general store, where he purchased new clothes, travel supplies, and other miscellaneous items for the trip to Reno. After arranging for a package to be delivered to the front desk of the International Hotel for Mia, he headed over to the livery stable, where his wagon would be secured, and his mules would be fed and boarded overnight.

Taking only his saddle bags and the scabbard containing the .44 Henry rifle with him, his next stop was a bathhouse, where he scrubbed what felt like a year's worth of sweat and dirt from his hair and body, and a quarter-inch of grime from beneath his fingernails before heading inside to the barber for a much-needed shave and haircut.

When he at last stepped outside into the evening air, he bore almost no resemblance to the scraggly miner who'd arrived in Virginia City earlier that day. He seemed more like a visiting businessman than a person who'd spent the past five years avoiding people by living only a degree or two removed from the life of a hermit.

In fact, there was only one person in all of Virginia City who would instantly recognize the stately stranger. It was already after 6:00 p.m. when he arrived at the gunsmith's shop, and after walking around the building to the residential entrance, he knocked firmly at the door.

From inside, he heard a somewhat irritated voice yelling out, "We close at 5:30 p.m., so I'll have to ask you to come back tomorrow."

To the right of the rear entrance, he saw the curtain move slightly, and five seconds later, the door flew open, and a surprised voice cried out, "Oliver!"

"Karen!" replied Oliver, opening his arms wide to welcome her into his embrace.

"You are a sight for sore eyes," she said, grinning from ear to ear while ushering him inside. Closing and locking the door behind him, she said, "Have a seat. I was just about to sit down for supper, and there was more than enough for both of us. Won't you join me?"

"I don't mind if I do," Oliver replied, taking a seat at the table as she filled another bowl with beef stew and cornbread and placed it in front of him.

After taking her seat, she blessed their food, and Oliver dug into what was his most delicious meal in recent memory. It had been years since his last visit, shortly after Karen's husband and Oliver's uncle, Jedediah, had passed away.

Following supper, while eyeing Oliver appreciatively as he sat there with a full stomach and a smile on his face, Karen asked, "What in Heaven's name are you doing in Virginia City?"

Leaning back in his chair and rubbing his belly, he said, "I had some business here earlier today, and in the morning, I'll be accompanying a young girl to the railroad station in Reno and then on to Boston."

"That wouldn't by chance be the Hampton girl, would it?" asked Karen.

"I'm not at liberty to say, but yes," answered Oliver. "Mia Hampton is her name."

"I heard that her parents were murdered on the way here, and she managed to wander into town after hiding from the killers and avoiding them all night," said Karen.

"She's a brave young lady," said Oliver. "She's been through Hell, but there's still a lot of fight left in her."

"She sounds a lot like you," Karen recalled. "When you showed up on our doorstep in San Antonio, you weren't much better off, but look at you now," she said. "Jedediah and I couldn't have been more proud of you."

"Well, in the morning I'll be taking her through some sketchy terrain, and my hardware could certainly use a tune-up," said Oliver.

"You know where everything is, so feel free to help yourself to whatever you need. Gun oil and cleaning supplies are on the shelf beneath the till, and if you need any replacement parts for that Peacemaker, you'll find them in the bottom drawer to the right of it," Karen explained, adding, "You can use the bunk upstairs in the loft tonight. There are extra blankets in the trunk at the foot of the bed, and I'll see you in the morning. "

"Thanks, Aunt Karen," said Oliver, hugging her again before she headed off to bed.

There were two advantages to sleeping in Aunt Karen's loft. First, it was directly across the street from the International Hotel, with a clear view of the building outside Mia's room, and second, no one would ever think to look for him there.

After carefully tending to his Colt and Derringer, he disassembled the Henry rifle, cleaning and inspecting the action thoroughly, before reassembling it and reloading all three weapons. Just as with tools specific to the mining trade, as a US marshal, reliable hardware was essential to his survival, and a single misfire could define the difference between life and death.

It was nearly 9:00 p.m. when Oliver put the tools and cleaning supplies away, extinguished the lanterns, and retired to his quarters upstairs in the loft. With everything in and around the International Hotel bathed in peace and quiet, after a challenging day, Oliver finally slept.

CHAPTER 4

DESPITE THE OBVIOUS challenges of the preceding two days, Mia had thoroughly enjoyed her stay at the International. She washed up with the fresh, clean water in the enormous pitcher and water basin, then wrapped herself in the impossibly large and soft bath towel, reluctant to put back on the dirty, tattered dress she'd worn earlier. Fortunately, the package Oliver had delivered for her arrived just in time and contained something she'd never worn before: store-bought clothes.

In addition to a flannel nightgown and fresh undergarments, there was a beautiful dress and ankle-boots that she absolutely adored, and another outfit she didn't particularly care for. There was also a comb, a hairbrush, a toothbrush, and a packet of red licorice. After dressing in her nightclothes, she was about to tear into the licorice when the room attendant knocked at the door, announcing they'd brought dinner for her.

For Mia, it felt almost as if she were dreaming. There were fresh vegetables and fried chicken with mashed potatoes and gravy; a basket of bread that was still warm from the oven; a tall glass of fresh milk; and a thick slice of apple pie for dessert. After eating as much of it as she could, she used some of the paper from the General Store packaging to wrap up the leftover bread and chicken, having opted to start with the slice of pie first.

Once she slipped between the crisp white bedsheets of the soft, comfortable bed, her head had barely touched the pillow before she fell asleep.

Across the street from the International Hotel, Oliver and Karen were already having breakfast. The smell of hot coffee, bacon, eggs, and Aunt Karen's signature caramel rolls drew Oliver out of bed and down the stairs well before 6:00 a.m., and following another delicious meal, he reluctantly said goodbye, promising to visit her again as soon as possible.

After collecting his mules and wagon from the livery stable, he parked out front and walked through the doors of the International shortly before 7:00 a.m., and had it not been for his extreme punctuality, the gentleman behind the reception desk would have drawn no correlation between him and the man he'd last seen only a few hours earlier.

"Good morning," he said, warmly greeting Oliver in sharp contrast to the dismissive attitude he'd displayed the previous afternoon. "It's nice to see you again, sir."

"Thank you," said Oliver, adding, "I trust everything was uneventful last night."

"As peaceful as could be, and our special guest is such a delightful child," he said. "This morning when the chamber maid took breakfast upstairs for her, she'd already made up her bed and washed and dried yesterday evening's dinnerware." Shaking his head in disbelief, he added, "In all my years, I've never seen any of our guests do such a thing, let alone a little girl."

"She's not a little girl," said Oliver. "She's almost eight, you know."

"Quite the young lady indeed," said the gentleman, nodding in acknowledgement, before disappearing into the office to retrieve Oliver's courier pouch.

After receiving it, he thanked the hospitality agent and headed upstairs to collect Mia, announcing himself before unlocking the door and entering the room. She was seated across from the door with her belongings gathered neatly around her, and was visibly shocked upon viewing Oliver's outward transformation.

Nevertheless, her first words were, "I hate it! I look like a boy!"

Mia was wearing bib overalls and a flannel shirt with lace-up Brogans and a boy's overcoat. The chamber maid had graciously helped her get dressed in the unfamiliar clothing, and despite her own obvious disdain,

Oliver's goal of altering her appearance had been quite effective. She really did look like a boy, and with her hair in a ponytail stuffed beneath the hat she was wearing, she bore absolutely no resemblance to the little girl who'd wandered into town the morning prior.

"It's only until we get to Reno," Oliver explained. "Then, you can wear your new dress and fancy boots on the train, all the way to Boston."

After collecting her things, Oliver took her hand, and the two of them headed down the stairs together. At the front desk, the chambermaid waved and said goodbye to Mia, and the reception clerk bid them both a fond farewell.

Once their guests had exited the lobby, the chamber maid said, "She's such a charming young girl," before asking, "Do you know where they're off to next?"

"No," the receptionist responded. "But wherever they're headed, it'd be best to stay out of their way."

"Why is that?" asked the puzzled woman, purely out of curiosity.

"Because that man with Mia is none other than Marshal Oliver Blackstone, and so far, no one who's ever called him out has lived to tell the tale." The man turned to face her and said, "And as far as we're concerned, they were never here."

"Who was never here?" asked the chamber maid, turning and walking away, neither expecting nor receiving an answer.

Outside, the streets were nearly deserted. Virginia City was no farming community, so early risers were an uncommon sight. By avoiding the main streets and thoroughfares, Oliver and Mia were able to slip out of town without encountering another living soul. By the time golden sunlight had chased away the morning gray blanketing the valley, Virginia City was little more than a mirage on the distant horizon.

Despite that fact, Oliver remained exceedingly alert, with nothing escaping his ever-watchful eyes. As they neared a familiar rise, approximately four miles into their journey, he spotted the wolf again. This time, she was alone with neither her cubs nor any coyotes in sight. She was simply standing there, peering out towards the northwestern ridge overlooking the well-traveled migration route between Reno and Virginia City.

At the crest of an elevated hillside in the distance, Oliver noticed a flash in the rocky terrain as sunlight glinted from the highly-polished surface of something moving there. Being quite some distance from the beaten path, it would take a while for it to become a threat to them, if it actually became a threat at all. He'd keep it in mind, but for the time being, his focus would remain on the potential pitfalls and ambush points in their immediate vicinity.

When he turned to look for the wolf again, she'd already vanished, but Oliver couldn't seem to shake the feeling that they would be seeing her again.

"She went that way," said Mia, seemingly preoccupied with the packet of licorice.

Looking over at her, Oliver asked, "Who went that way?"

"The big dog with the puppies," said Mia, biting off another piece of the chewy candy while looking up at him.

Oliver squinted curiously, but didn't say a word.

Once she'd finished chewing, as if it were the most normal thing in the world, Mia said, "She took me to the city the night my mom and dad..."

For a moment, her voice trailed off as if she were reliving that painfully tragic event, but after regaining her composure, she continued, saying, "She chased away the other dog, and then I followed her down the road until I saw the city."

After hearing her side of the story, the pieces of an unsolved puzzle came together in Oliver's mind. That other dog had been a coyote, and the wolf hadn't chased it away. She'd killed it.

Whether by coincidence or some other grand design, Mia had been afforded a capable guardian angel on her way into Virginia City. Now she was leaving it seated beside a man formerly known as the Grim Reaper. In either case, the coyotes stalking them had best beware.

They had already been underway for nearly two hours before the first travelers could be seen approaching in the distance.

As they drew nearer, it was obvious that they posed no threat to either Oliver or Mia. They were simply a tired family of four with a few miles to go before reaching the end of their journey. However, as the wagons passed in a small valley between two rolling hills, the looks on their faces were not those of weary travelers, but rather those of a family fearing for their lives.

When the man holding the reins removed and tipped his hat, the look in his eyes was sincerely apologetic. It was at that moment when Oliver realized he was confirming that the second passenger in the wagon was a girl.

Oliver wasn't even upset with the man. Securing safe passage for his own beloved family at the price of betraying a total stranger on a desolate road only a few miles from their final destination of Virginia City? It was a deal any reasonable husband and father would have made to protect their wife and children, especially when considering the consequences of refusing such an offer.

Without revealing that he'd spied the posted spotter attempting to scurry unnoticed back over the hilltop ahead of them, Oliver slowed the pace of his mules, stalling for time and allowing the family they had just passed to reach and cross beyond the crest of the hill behind them.

Once the other wagon was no longer in the line of fire, Oliver told Mia, "I'm going to stop up ahead beside those two large rocks and the sagebrush. When I do, I want you to climb down and wait there until I come back for you, okay?"

"Do you promise you'll come back for me?" asked Mia, her eyes wide with apprehension.

"I promise," said Oliver, winking to reassure her.

A few seconds later, the wagon stopped, and Mia hopped down, taking cover as Oliver had instructed. Afterwards, he brought the mules to a brisk trot before releasing the reins and laying down on his back in the bed of the wagon with the rifle clutched to his chest. The mules would continue to follow the road at that pace either until they were tired or slowed by someone taking the reins to stop them.

When they reached the apex of the hill and headed down the slope, Oliver could hear horses approaching from both sides, but waited until he could see the sharpshooter on the hillside before sitting up in the bed of the wagon. The sound of the Henry rang out, echoing across the hillside as the man holding the Winchester dropped to the ground, vanishing into the tall yellow grass.

When the wagon appeared on the hilltop, the mounted gunmen hesitated, believing it to be empty. By the time they recognized the oversight, their five-to-one odds had been cut to two-to-one, and the two riders approaching from the right toppled from their horses when that Henry rifle roared twice more.

With over half of their assassin squad already bleeding out into the fertile Nevada topsoil, this self-proclaimed band of raiders had quickly devolved into a duo of worthless braggarts, wondering which of them would be the next to die. When their horses sensed the waning confidence of their riders, firing haphazardly into the empty space around them, they literally revolted, bucking wildly in an attempt to rid themselves of the excess baggage preventing them from running for the hills in the opposite direction.

Oliver was happy to assist in clearing their saddles for them, and when his Henry rifle issued two additional proclamations, the verdict was guilty, and the sentence was death.

Mia waited nervously right where Oliver had hidden her, and when the shooting started, she closed her eyes tightly and covered her ears. It was over far sooner than she'd expected, but after the final shots rang out, she was much too afraid to even venture a glance from behind the rocks, and continued sitting there quietly with her eyes closed.

She waited there for several tense minutes and nearly jumped out of her skin when she felt a hand gently touch her shoulder. She opened her eyes to find Oliver smiling down at her, and literally sprang to her feet and leapt into his arms.

"You really came back for me," she said, excitedly.

"I promised you that I would," Oliver replied, gently lowering her to the ground and taking her hand.

As the two of them walked up the hill to where the mules and the wagon were waiting, Mia looked up at him, quizzically furrowing her brow and asking, "Did you tell them your name?"

After a brief pause, Oliver huffed slightly and said, "I suppose I did."

CHAPTER 5

EDWIN MEYERS WAS actually surprised himself when he and his family made it to the outskirts of Virginia City. He was certain they were nothing more than walking dead after leaving the band of outlaws who'd detained and threatened them. Whether it was the bandits who came to eliminate them as witnesses or the man in the wagon with the child, to exact his revenge on them, Edwin never expected to make it into Virginia City.

When he did, his first stop was directly outside the sheriff's office, where he roused a still-sleeping Sheriff Walsh to report the incident. The sheriff had been up long into the night, keeping an eye on the obviously trigger-happy gunslingers wandering the bounty of Virginia City Saloons, apparently in search of the gunman who'd taken down Blink Masterson.

"He was a tall, clean-shaven fella wearing a black broadcloth suit," Edwin explained. "The child with him looked like a boy at first, wearing bib overalls and clod-hoppers, but when we got closer, I could see it was the girl those men were looking for."

"And you just gave them up... without even trying to warn them?" asked the sheriff, judgmentally.

"Well, what was I supposed to do?" countered Edwin, albeit remorsefully. "I could feel the crosshairs of that Winchester on the back of my head the entire time, and my only way out of that valley was to keep my mouth shut and tip my hat if I saw the girl. Hell, they'd be coming after us anyway, no matter what I did. I had to at least try to protect my family. "

"I can't say I'd fault you for that," said Sheriff Walsh, after some thoughtful consideration. "Do you know how many bandits there were?" he asked.

"Well," said Edwin. "There was the sharpshooter on the hill, and four others who rode up from both sides of the road when we approached." Looking up and to the left, he pursed his lips in deep reflection before saying, "I think that was all of them, but it wasn't long after that when we heard the shooting start, and I brought old Chester and Nelly here to a gallop, and got us the hell outta there as fast as possible."

"Shooting?" repeated the sheriff. "As in, more than one shot?" he queried.

"Yessir," said Edwin. "There were maybe ten or twelve shots; most of them were rifle fire with a few pistol rounds mixed in with them, but the last one was definitely from a rifle."

"At least they put up a fight," said Sheriff Walsh. "Hopefully, he was able to wing one of them bad enough for him to need a doctor. If so, I'm sure at least one will be slinking into town around dusk, if he can hold out that long."

"That little girl wasn't hurting anybody!" said Mildred, angrily. "She was just sitting there, chewing on her licorice, and minding her own business. The poor child could have been one of my own, and those animals probably just gunned her down in cold blood," she stated, adding, "I hope they all hang!"

Walking up the wooden steps, Sheriff Walsh started ringing the bell mounted on the wall just outside the jailhouse. Within minutes, several deputies arrived, most of whom seemed just as tired as the sheriff.

"Jimmy, I need you and the boys to ride out to Primrose Peak," ordered Sheriff Walsh. "Evidently, there's been another ambush out that way, and I need you to find the victims, and see if there's anything that can be done for them, even if that just means bringing back the bodies for a proper burial."

"You got it, sheriff," said Jimmy, as he and the other men dispersed momentarily to retrieve their horses. Within minutes, the posse of seven men had left Virginia City and were galloping northwest towards Primrose Peak.

After taking Edwin's and Mildred's sworn statements, Sheriff Walsh told them that they could be on their way, adding, "Welcome to Virginia City."

While the deputies were underway to recover the bodies of the victims, Sheriff Walsh was feeling highly unsettled by the events of the past few days. Why a wealthy US marshal would suddenly befriend an orphaned child with whom he had no discernable connection was perplexing to him.

First of all, he couldn't understand why the Hamptons had been targeted in the first place. They weren't wealthy travelers heading in from Reno and looking to stake their claim in Virginia City. Like so many others, they were a family of prospectors hoping to carve out a living for themselves in the rapidly expanding western frontier.

By whatever miracle had aided Mia in reaching Virginia City, it was now clear that she'd seen whoever had killed her parents, making her a loose end that needed to be tended to. Whether he had been operating on his own or in the interest of an undisclosed third party, Blink Masterson had certainly not expected to be outdrawn by some mangy prospector who literally no one had ever even seen in Virginia City before.

Even Frederick Walsh had questioned the veracity of the filthy vagrant, who'd claimed to be a US marshal, and having been Virginia City's sheriff for only three years, the name Oliver Blackstone meant nothing to him.

He was unaware the unlikely duo had even left the city, believing they were still holed-up somewhere, waiting for things to settle down a bit before embarking on their journey back to Boston. However, Mildred Meyer's emotional outburst had provided Sheriff Walsh with a clue previously unknown to him.

The little girl had been eating licorice when she was last seen, and the sheriff suspected that it had been purchased along with her boyish clothing at the nearby General Store. Although that establishment received a large volume of walk-in business each day, the number of men who'd purchased new clothing for themselves and a little boy, along with a package of licorice candy, would almost certainly reduce that number to one.

Lars and Eva Madsen remembered the man immediately, with Eva explaining, "He spent forty-two dollars in only a few minutes. Some of it was for a little boy, but most of it was for a girl. You know... brushes and unmentionables, a nightgown, and the prettiest dress we had in the store. He also bought a new shirt, some socks, and long johns for himself and the suit on the mannequin in the window." Nodding towards her husband, she said, "He was rather slender, so Lars took in the waist, lowered the cuffs on the trousers, and adjusted the sleeves on the coat, then delivered everything across the street to the bathhouse for him."

"Not everything," started Lars before being cut off by a rather talkative Eva.

"That's right," she continued, saying, "My husband took the items he purchased for the children over to the International Hotel and dropped them off at the reception desk," Eva concluded, while nodding at Lars, as if to inform him that he had nothing else she needed to say for him.

"You forgot the ankle boots," Lars muttered under his breath.

"I didn't forget them," said Eva, shooting a reprimanding glance in Lars' direction. "I simply hadn't mentioned them yet."

"Did either of you happen to get his name?" asked the sheriff.

"He never mentioned his name," said Eva. "But, the package for the International Hotel, including a pair of ankle boots... was addressed to Mia Hampton," Eva concluded, shooting another admonishing glance in her husband's direction.

"Well, thank you kindly," said the sheriff, tipping his hat and leaving the store with the sound of Eva Madsen's irksome voice accompanying him out onto the sidewalk as she vociferously chastised her husband Lars for embarrassing her.

Instead of retracing every step the marshal/prospector had made, Sheriff Walsh proceeded directly to the International Hotel, where he was warmly greeted at the reception desk.

"Good afternoon, Sheriff Walsh," said the man with a smile.

"Good afternoon, Alfred," the sheriff said, extending his arm for a handshake.

"What brings Virginia City's finest to our doorstep on this lovely day?" queried Alfred.

"I'm just trying to make some sense of the past few days," the sheriff replied, adding, "I was hoping you could help me out."

Alfred replied, "Whatever I can do for the sake of law and order, you need only ask."

"Yesterday afternoon, there was a package delivered here for Mia Hampton," said the sheriff. "I was wondering if you could tell me with whom she was registered."

"With as many people flowing into Virginia City due to the Comstock Lode, it's nearly impossible to keep track of all our guests," said Alfred, apparently having difficulty recalling either the girl or the package.

"Do you mind if I have a look at the guest register?" asked Sheriff Walsh. "Maybe that will shed some light on the details and possibly jog your memory."

"That would be highly irregular, Sheriff Walsh," Alfred protested. "Our guests are accustomed to a certain degree of privacy while residing with us, and I'd be exceedingly uncomfortable revealing that information without their expressed consent."

"Unfortunately, that may no longer be possible," said the sheriff. Looking into Alfred's eyes, he explained, "I've got a posse headed out to Primrose Peak as we speak. Some travelers they passed on the way into Virginia City believe they may have been killed in an ambush out there this morning. "

Behind him, a porcelain water carafe shattered loudly against the decorative marble floor, and the sheriff turned sharply to find the chamber maid, Annette, standing there with both hands covering her face.

With tears flooding her eyes, she screamed, "No!" before turning and running from the lobby.

Pivoting back towards Alfred, Sheriff Walsh said, "Perhaps I should be speaking with her instead."

Taking the sheriff's arm and ushering him into the office behind the reception desk, Alfred nervously admitted, "Yes, the young lady did spend the night here; however, the reservation was in her name, and she was absolutely alone in the room for the entire evening."

"And no one came to visit her after she checked in?" asked the sheriff.

Alfred explained that from the time she checked in until she left, no one other than him or Anette went up to her room, and they were only there to bring her dinner last evening and breakfast earlier that morning.

Clearly unconvinced, the sheriff asked, "Well, how did she get here, and who paid for the room?" While he suspected he knew the answers to all of those questions, he wasn't willing to reveal the extent of his own knowledge until he knew how all of the pieces fit together.

Sighing deeply, Alfred finally admitted, "There was a man with her when she checked in, late yesterday afternoon."

"Do you happen to remember his name?" asked the sheriff.

"He neither asked for mine nor offered me his," Alfred replied. "I assumed he'd chosen to remain anonymous for a reason."

"And was it the same man who picked her up this morning?" asked Sheriff Walsh.

"It was," Alfred replied, adding, "although his appearance was certainly more distinguished than it had been yesterday afternoon."

"Thank you," said the sheriff, turning to leave the office as Alfred reached for the broom and dustpan propped in the corner next to the exit. Before crossing the lobby to the front door, Sheriff Walsh stopped and asked, "By the way, does the name Oliver Blackstone ring any bells?"

Alfred froze on the spot, and turned slowly to face the sheriff, saying, "You mean... It doesn't mean anything to you?"

"No," replied the sheriff, before asking, "Why? Should it?"

Slowly walking towards him, Alfred said, "Between 1860 and 1870, Marshal Oliver Blackstone collected more bounties and brought more murderous outlaws to justice than the next ten US marshals combined, and he was the first marshal in US history to have a bounty placed on his own head by the fugitives running from him; a bounty totaling more than one-hundred-thousand dollars."

Now standing face-to-face with the sheriff, Alfred said, "If Mia Hampton is traveling with Marshal Oliver Blackstone, it won't be their bodies your deputies bring back from Primrose Peak. Someone out there has resurrected the goddamned devil, and now... they're all going straight to Hell. "

CHAPTER 6

BEFORE WALKING BACK down the road to Mia's hiding spot, Oliver collected the bodies of their would-be assailants, lined them up neatly in a row, and covered them with their bedrolls. He also rounded up and staked down the horses near the road using a rope from one of the saddles, making it easy for the sheriff and his men to locate them.

By the time he and Mia reached the wagon, there was nothing visible that would further scar her childhood or add to the nightmares she'd already endured. After less than a half-hour delay, they were back on the road, with Primrose Peak rapidly fading into a distant memory.

"What's your wife's name?" asked Mia, quite unexpectedly.

Somewhat taken aback by the question, Oliver said, "Her name is Sarah, but we're not married yet."

"Why not?" asked Mia.

"Well, she's still in Boston, and I plan to ask her as soon as I get back there," Oliver explained.

Squinting up at him, apparently confused, Mia asked, "How come she's in Boston, and you're way out here?"

Smiling more to himself than to Mia, Oliver replied, "I guess I wanted to offer her something meaningful before we tied the knot."

"And you're not good enough?" she asked.

"It's not like that," said Oliver. "It's just that when you love someone, you want to be able to take care of them and make sure they have all the things they need."

"What kind of things?" Mia pried, insistently.

"You know, things like a house and a quiet little piece of land in the countryside, where you can raise a family. Maybe even some horses or livestock. Things like that," said Oliver in deep reflection.

"My dad built our house," said Mia. "We had a big yard and a tree with a swing in it, and a milk cow named Mae, in the barn with the horses."

"That sounds really nice," replied Oliver, smiling down at her.

"It was until the water slowed down." Mia explained. "Then, everything started to go dry, and we didn't have enough water for Dad to pan the gold anymore."

"Why did the water slow down?" asked Oliver, genuinely curious.

"Dad said that Mister Kasey's dam was stopping the water, so he went there and tore it down, and then the water came back. But then Mister Kasey got really mad and made the dam even bigger and hired men with guns to keep Dad away from it. After that, there was only water from the well for us," Mia explained.

"What did your dad do when that happened?" asked Oliver.

Mia explained, "Mister Kasey wanted to buy our land, but Mom and Dad wouldn't sell it to him, so he got mad again and sent people to burn down the barn." Continuing, she said, "Since there was no water in the stream anymore, we couldn't put out the fire, and we lost Mae. We were going into town so Dad could tell the sheriff about it, but Mister Kasey's men followed us and...

"It's all right," said Oliver, giving Mia a moment before asking, "Do you think you would recognize those men who were chasing you?"

"I think so," said Mia. "I remember the one who tried to shoot you in town," she said.

"You mean, that was one of the men working for Mister Kasey?" Oliver clarified.

"Yes," said Mia. "He was the one who chased me, but it was getting dark, and when I hid inside the little cave with the puppies, I stayed really quiet, and he couldn't find me."

"You're a resourceful young lady," noted Oliver, smiling at her.

Furrowing her brow, Mia asked, "What's re... sore full?"

"Resourceful," Oliver said, "It means you're smart and clever and someone who can figure out how to make things work for them."

"Oh," said Mia, nodding contemplatively.

"So, other than that man in Virginia City, did you see anyone else you would remember from that evening?" Oliver inquired.

"I think some of them were riding the horses we passed back there by the road," Mia noted. "But the man who shot Mom and Dad was riding a shiny black horse and had a saddle with fancy silver buttons on it."

Raising his eyebrows in admiration, Oliver said, "With a memory like yours, it's no wonder why they're all afraid of you."

"But I'm just a girl," said Mia. "I don't even have a gun, so why would anybody be afraid of me?"

"Because you have something much better than a gun," said Oliver, tapping his forehead with his index finger. "You're smart and you notice things that most people don't even see."

"Mom used to say that I ask too many questions," said Mia.

"Well, if you don't ask the questions, you'll never know the answers," said Oliver.

"Did you ever ask Sarah to marry you?" inquired Mia.

"Not directly," said Oliver.

"Why not?" Mia asked.

"Because I asked her father, and he said no," Oliver replied.

"Why would you ask her father to marry you?" pondered Mia. "That doesn't sound very resourceful."

"You know," said Oliver, chuckling aloud, "you do ask an awful lot of questions."

"Would you like some fried chicken?" Mia offered, magically producing the leftovers from her assortment of packages and belongings.

"Where did you..." started Oliver, before simply saying, "Yes please."

With that, their conversation ended, and the two of them enjoyed an unexpected lunch while continuing along their journey.

Despite being surrounded by the pristine wilderness of Northern Nevada, during daylight, the roadway connecting Reno and Virginia City was a commonly utilized one. By noon, there were a multitude of travelers bound for destinations along that route, including a veritable army of Wells Fargo agents and federal couriers, hired to ensure the safe, uninterrupted flow of money, title documents, and precious metals throughout the region.

With little opportunity for bandits and outlaws to exploit hapless commuters until after dusk, the remainder of the journey was uneventful for Oliver and Mia. Upon reaching Reno, Marshal Blackstone immediately reported the incident at Primrose Peak to the regional US Marshals Service field office there, along with the testimony taken from Mia Hampton, pertaining to the murder of her parents.

Handing the deputy marshal the signed affidavit from Virginia City, Oliver advised him that, as her lawful guardian, duly authorized by Sheriff Walsh in Virginia City, he would be escorting Miss Hampton back to Boston in order to reunite her with her next-of-kin. Should their investigation lead to an arrest requiring her witness testimony, Mia would return.

The deputy marshal handed him back the document from Virginia City and said, "Welcome back to active service, Marshal Blackstone."

Once the official portion of his responsibilities had been reported and documented, he left the field office wearing his US Marshals Service badge, displayed prominently on his lapel.

Their next stop was the Western Union telegraph office. After penning an urgent message to Sarah Hutchins, he handed it to the telegraph agent.

Reading it aloud for confirmation, the agent repeated, "Departure delayed by 24 hours (stop). I am the official travel guardian for Mia Hampton, age 7 (stop). Leaving Reno at 10:30 a.m. and arriving in Boston in 7 days (stop). I love you and miss you dearly (full stop). "

"Full stop?" asked Mia. "You forgot to ask her to marry you," she said, looking up at Oliver expectantly.

"That's not something you do in a wire dispatch," said Oliver, looking sheepishly at the telegraph agent.

"Why not? Don't you want to marry her?" asked Mia, insistently.

Squeezing her hand, Oliver looked down at her affectionately and said, "Of course I do!"

"Then ask her," said Mia, adding, "If you don't ask the question, you'll never know the answer."

When Oliver looked up at the telegraph agent again, he was standing there, fountain pen in hand, seemingly eager to add another line to the dispatch.

Tugging his hand and drawing Oliver's attention back to her, Mia said solemnly, "Not everything can wait for a week."

As Oliver stood there, the past few years of his life seemed to replay in rapid succession. Since meeting Sarah, he'd asked her for many things, not the least of which being for her to put her life on hold for five years while he left her alone in Boston and headed out west.

Suddenly, it occurred to him. When he'd asked her to give him five years, she didn't hesitate because she doubted him. She hesitated because she was hoping he would propose and take her with him.

"You're right," said Oliver, following an unexpectedly long pause. "Not everything can wait for another week, or even another day." Taking the fountain pen and paper from the telegraph agent, he amended the content, reading it aloud, saying, "I love and miss you dearly (stop). Will you marry me? (Full stop)."

A spattering of applause filled the tiny telegraph office, and he turned to find several smiling patrons were clapping their hands in approval. There was also one matronly woman standing directly behind him, dabbing the corners of her eyes with a linen handkerchief, who said with a trembling voice, "Young man, that was so beautiful!"

Upon receiving confirmation from the telegraph agent that the dispatch had been sent, Oliver and a smiling Mia left the Western Union office, climbed back aboard the mule-drawn wagon, and continued down the street to the Frontier Hotel.

In Virginia City, Frederick Walsh was still puzzling over the neatly-packaged corpses discovered by his deputies at Primrose Peak. Each of them had matching potato-sized exit wounds from a .44 Henry rifle, and an official

US marshal calling card bearing the name Oliver Blackstone was discovered inside the shirt pockets of each body collected.

According to the testimony of Edwin Meyers, these men had Marshal Blackstone and Mia Hampton dead to rights, and it was inconceivable to the sheriff how they could have gotten out alive. Perhaps Marshal Blackstone really was the Devil, but if so, he was certainly sinking his pitchfork into the most unsavory of characters.

With the telegraph from the US Marshals Service field office in Reno connecting Blink Masterson to the Hampton Murder and implicating Clifford Kasey, the entire case seemed to be devolving into nothing more than a dispute between two neighboring landowners over contested water rights. Still, without concrete evidence tying Clifford Kasey to the men who'd murdered Donovan and Beverly Hampton, the assertions of a seven-year-old girl wouldn't hold much weight in a court of law.

On the other hand, if he could find the man Mia had witnessed murdering her parents, that would be a different matter altogether. Outlaws aren't typically known for their generosity, and when it comes to risking their own necks, they seldom work for free.

If Sheriff Walsh were going to make the case against a man as influential as Clifford Kasey and connect him to the men who'd killed Mia's parents, then he would have to use the same tactics as the outlaws and bandits operating on the western frontier. He would simply follow the money.

CHAPTER 7

WHEN MIA EMERGED from her room and walked down the stairway ahead of a smiling chamber maid and into the busy restaurant of the Frontier Hotel, an obvious hush fell over the crowded dining hall. Upon seeing her, Marshal Blackstone rose to his feet, walking around the table to pull out a chair for her.

Wearing the outfit Oliver had purchased in Virginia City, Mia looked as if she'd stepped right from the pages of a fairy tale book. The chamber maid, Annie, had bathed her in floral-scented soap and washed her hair before drying and brushing it out for her. After dressing Mia in her brand-new bloomers and ruffled socks, Annie helped her into the pastel pink dress, showing her how to connect all of the decorative hooks and eyelets running down the front of it.

After her prolonged anticipation, Mia was finally able to slip into the polished leather ankle-boots she'd been swooning over since first seeing them. Once they were properly laced and tied, Annie stood Mia in front of the full-length mirror inside her room.

"I swear that you are the most precious thing I have ever seen," Annie declared, standing behind Mia to admire her own handiwork. "Now for the finishing touches," she said, slipping a pair of satin dinner gloves onto Mia's hands and carefully positioning a matching decorative hat atop her head.

"You are truly a living doll!" Annie exclaimed, pinching Mia's cheeks to give her face a burst of color, before following her out of the room and down the stairs as if she were a princess.

Upon reaching the table and being seated, Oliver returned to his seat directly across from her, saying, "Well, you certainly don't look like a boy anymore."

"Do you like it?" Mia asked, excitedly. "I love it!" she blurted out before Oliver could even open his mouth to express his agreement.

In the 1870s, it was highly unusual to see a child seated in a restaurant, and despite the obvious excitement of wearing her new outfit, Mia was, herself, somewhat uncomfortable dining there. That discomfort was further exacerbated when the waitress placed her meal in front of her, amidst an assortment of various forks, spoons, and knives, with which Mia was completely unfamiliar.

Although she was clearly eager to devour the vegetables, mashed potatoes, and gravy, and the sizzling porkchop in front of her, Mia had never used any dining utensils other than a simple spoon. Her mother had always cut the meat on her plate into bite-sized morsels for her, and Mia was clearly at a loss in this highly formal environment.

Noticing Mia's obvious awkwardness, the affable waitress calmly gathered the needless array of confusing silverware and dropped it into the pocket of her apron. Then, using a fork and knife, she deftly cut the porkchop into smaller pieces before placing one fork and one spoon on either side of Mia's plate.

"Thank you," said Mia, smiling up at her.

"You're welcome, sweetheart," the waitress replied, before leaning in and whispering, "Most of it's for show anyway."

Even while wearing the garb of a trust-fund child, Mia remained the polite yet inquisitive young girl her parents had raised her to be. Before getting started, she asked, "Oliver, do I have to wear the gloves while I'm eating?"

"Not unless you want to," Oliver replied.

"They make it hard to hold onto anything," said Mia, removing them and placing them neatly on the table next to her. She tucked the cloth napkin into the neckline of her dress and smoothed it out over her clothes before finally commencing with her meal.

Despite the odd looks they attracted from some of the guests seated around them, Mia and Oliver enjoyed their meal together, oblivious to the muted murmurings of a room filled with strangers. After splitting an oversized slice of cherry pie, Mia was both full and tired, and once he'd settled their tab, Oliver motioned to Annie, asking her to escort Mia back up to her room for the evening.

Pulling out the chair for her, Oliver said, "Goodnight, Mia. I'll see you in the morning. "

"Goodnight, Oliver," Mia replied, adding, "Thank you for everything," as Annie took her hand and walked her up the stairs.

It was still relatively early, and with him and Mia departing the next morning, Oliver walked across the street to the livery stable, where he negotiated a fair price of fifty dollars for both of his mules and the wagon.

As he was headed back across the street to the hotel, he heard a voice call out to him, saying, "Hey mister."

Looking back over his shoulder while placing the assorted denominations of bills into the inside breast pocket of his coat, Oliver said, "Yes?"

The man standing there said, "People told me that you're the fellow who..." His voice trailed off when Oliver completed his turn, facing him with his marshal's badge on full display.

"The fellow who what?" asked Oliver.

"Oh, excuse me, marshal," said the man, apologetically adding, "My mistake," while tipping his hat and walking off in the direction of the saloon a few doors further down along the wooden walkway.

Keeping the stranger under observation until it was obvious he wouldn't be returning; Oliver was about to resume his stroll back to the hotel when another figure came trotting towards him from across the street.

"Marshal!" shouted the man, excitedly waving a familiar pale-yellow, folded sheet of paper over his head. Oliver recognized the Western Union telegraph agent as he drew nearer, saying, "I have an urgent dispatch for you from Boston, and I was just on my way to deliver it to your hotel."

Taking the piece of paper, Oliver extended the telegraph agent a silver dollar, saying, "Thank you."

"Oh, I couldn't," said the smiling man, tossing up his hands and winking before turning and heading back across the street towards the Western Union office.

As Oliver held the dispatch, he noticed his hands were actually shaking. This marshal, who could stare down the deadliest men on the western frontier without so much as batting an eye, was now as nervous as a schoolboy.

Pensively unfolding the message and reading Sarah's reply, it said, "My beloved Oliver (stop). I'm thrilled to hear you will soon be back in Boston (stop). I am anxious to meet

Mia (stop). Of course, I will marry you (stop). I adore you and I shall never (stop). Forever yours and impatiently awaiting your return, Sarah (Full Stop). "

Oliver didn't know whether to scream or pass out, opting instead to just sit down on the bench outside the entrance of the hotel. His mind was racing as he realized just how close he was to achieving his most treasured dream.

As he sat there, breathing in the cool evening air, and listening to the unmistakable song of a northern mockingbird welcoming nightfall, he heard the sound of a rider approaching from an alleyway intersecting the main thoroughfare.

A few seconds later, the stranger who'd approached him only minutes earlier appeared astride a beautiful shiny black mare. Before they disappeared into the surrounding darkness, Oliver caught only a glimpse of the rider's saddle and saddlebags, adorned with an abundance of garish silver studs.

"Son of a bitch," muttered Oliver, immediately springing to his feet although fully aware that it would have been pointless to try and pursue the rider on foot.

"You may have slipped past me this time, but now I know who you are." As his eyes and ears followed the sound of the horse's hooves fading into the distance, Oliver said, "Next time... you won't be so lucky."

As he turned and walked back into the hotel, he crossed the lobby, making his way over to the far end of the bar opposite the entrance to the restaurant.

The smiling barkeep approached, asking, "What can I get you, marshal?"

"Rye whiskey," Oliver replied.

"That sounds like a celebration to me," said the barkeep. "A glass or a bottle?" he asked.

"A glass will be fine," said Oliver.

Placing a tumbler in front of Oliver and filling it, he said, "What's the occasion, if you don't mind me asking?"

"Well, I just got engaged," said Oliver, raising his glass and saying, "Cheers!"

"Congratulations," said the smiling barkeep, reaching out to shake Oliver's hand and saying, "This one's on the house!"

After pouring himself a glass and toasting with the marshal, he asked, "Have you told your daughter yet?"

"I don't... Not yet," he said, downing the whiskey before leaving a half-dollar on the bar and heading upstairs to turn in for the night.

CHAPTER 8

"THE MAN IS a federal marshal," said Charlie Spurlock. "I can't just call him out and claim we had a disagreement at the poker table!"

"I don't care if he's the damned Secretary of State!" screamed Clifford Kasey. "I paid for a clean job with no witnesses, and you left behind the biggest witness of them all." On top of that, as long as she's still alive, that parcel of land will go to her, rather than end up on the state auction block. "

"I already told you; I don't kill children, and it's not my fault your man, Masterson, failed to get the job done," stated Spurlock.

"And I told you; you don't need to kill her. Just get rid of the man traveling with her, and bring her back here to me," insisted Clifford. "Aren't you supposed to be the Washoe Kid? It wouldn't be very beneficial for your reputation if word got out that *you* couldn't get the job done either. "

"Are you calling me out?" asked Spurlock, slowly lowering his hand to his side and turning to face Clifford Kasey.

The clicking sounds from the hammers of two double-barreled shotguns pointed at the back of his head quickly discouraged Spurlock from further escalating the situation.

"Listen," said Kasey. "No one is threatening you. I'm just asking you to hold up your end of the bargain. What difference does it make if the man is a US marshal or not? If that little girl identifies you as the killer who put bullets into the backs of Donovan and Beverly Hampton, you're going to hang anyway."

Stepping towards Spurlock, Clifford stated, "I'm actually paying you another thousand dollars to handle a situation that's in both our interests to resolve as quickly as possible."

Reaching into his inner coat pocket, Spurlock drew another nervous reaction from the two gunmen covering him. Withdrawing his hand slowly and deliberately, he was holding the envelope of cash that Clifford had given him earlier that day. Placing it on the table near the front door, he said, "I'll handle my own problems, and you... can handle yours."

Looking back at Clifford, Spurlock said, "That girl is boarding a train to Boston a few hours from now, and it's unlikely that I'll ever see her again." He turned back to the door and added, "It seems to me that your problem is a hell of a lot bigger than mine."

With that, Spurlock left the house without even bothering to close the door, mounted his horse, and trotted off into the darkness from which he'd come.

"That smug son of a bitch!" shouted Clifford, snatching the envelope from the table and kicking the door shut.

As much as he hated to admit it, Spurlock was right. As long as Mia Hampton was on the other side of the country, he had little to fear. On the other hand, as long as she was still alive, whether in Nevada or in Massachusetts, that land parcel would belong to her in perpetuity, and any attempt Clifford Kasey made to acquire it, either legally or otherwise, would only bring a landslide of suspicion crashing down on him.

Suddenly, it occurred to him. As long as Mia wasn't actually living on the land, Kasey could gradually appropriate it an acre at a time, and with no one there to challenge his access rights to the property, he would basically absorb it into his own within a year or two.

It was an excellent plan. In fact, it probably would have even worked had Sheriff Walsh not been monitoring the traffic in and out of the Kasey ranch since shortly before sunset. He figured it was only a matter of time before that shiny black horse with the fancy silver buttons showed up there to either call, raise, or fold.

Although he wasn't prepared to attempt singlehandedly arresting a professional gunslinger in the middle of the night, his primary objective had been to prove a connection between Clifford Kasey and the alleged killer. Now that he'd done so, it was simply a matter of applying pressure in the right places until leaks started to spring and the rats began to flee a sinking ship.

Unlike Marshal Blackstone, Frederick Walsh had earned his stripes while employed with the Pinkerton Detective Agency in Chicago, Illinois, beginning in 1858. In 1861, while working undercover to gather evidence on a plan by Southern sympathizers to sabotage the rail lines to Washington, D.C., Detective Walsh, and his team unveiled a plot to assassinate President-elect Abraham Lincoln.

Due to their decisive actions in rescheduling the president-elect's travel arrangements and disabling the telegraph lines to prevent the ill-willed actors from relaying the information regarding the change, Lincoln arrived safely in Washington the following morning, and a major disaster was avoided. However, with his cover as an undercover detective blown, he left Chicago and the Pinkerton agency in search of greener pastures. After a number of years working as an independent private detective, he eventually landed a temporary appointment as interim sheriff in Virginia City, Nevada, and was officially elected to the office one year later.

In a place like Virginia City, his style of preventative law enforcement found fertile ground as opposed to the reactionary style of the former sheriff, whose "rushing in with guns blazing" approach had ended abruptly during an ambush in an abandoned alleyway.

Sheriff Walsh discovered that by keeping his deputies engaged in the city's underground information network, he could address potential problems before they became critical and diffuse situations before they escalated into deadly confrontations. It was a strategy that had served the citizens of Virginia City well prior to the recent cold-blooded murders of Donovan and Beverly Hampton.

It was a situation that the detective in him simply couldn't permit to go unresolved. As he gathered the evidence that would hopefully bring justice and closure to this tragedy of horrors, his sights were set on the suspect who'd set those wheels into motion, because even a man such as Clifford Kasey was not above the law, and if he were guilty, he was going down.

The next morning, after a rejuvenating night's sleep and a bountiful breakfast, Marshal Oliver Blackstone and Mia Hampton boarded the Union Pacific Railroad's passenger train, bound for Boston, Massachusetts.

Following the unexpected appearance of the man suspected of murdering Mia's parents,

Oliver remained exceptionally vigilant, closely monitoring the actions of everyone around them. Nevertheless, deeming it an unnecessary distraction for Mia, he decided not to tell her about the previous evening's encounter.

Once the train left the station and they were finally underway, Oliver relaxed, joining Mia in marveling at the magnificent view of the passing landscapes through the amply sized passenger windows of the first-class Pullman car. While admiring the grandeur of the American West, Oliver thought fondly of Sarah, wishing she could have been there to experience it with him.

As if reading his thoughts, Mia asked, "Have you heard from Sarah yet?"

"As a matter of fact, I have," said Oliver, with a smile that unambiguously revealed the summary of her reply. However, at Mia's insistence, he read the letter aloud, word-for-word, then repeated it to her again for good measure.

"I knew she would say yes," stated Mia confidently.

"How could you have known that?" asked Oliver, chuckling aloud, and saying, "You've never even met her."

"But I've met you," said Mia, returning her full attention to the scenery passing outside the window without further explanation.

Oddly, at that moment, it struck Oliver that he'd only known Mia for three days. In another week, she would be back in Boston with her relatives, and his legal responsibility for her guardianship would end.

While he was genuinely happy for her and the upcoming reunion with her family, after five years of self-imposed isolation, he'd spent more time with Mia than he had with anyone else during that entire period. Admittedly, he had grown quite fond of her, and was now more determined than ever to get her safely back home to her family.

After a few hours, the excitement began to ebb, and Mia expectedly drifted off to sleep. Oliver pulled out and re-read the telegram from Sarah several more times before retrieving the US Marshals Service purse from his travel bag and opening it.

Inside, there were a number of different documents, such as the deeds for both his properties in Massachusetts and Nevada; a meticulously maintained balance booklet for his private banking account; a few of his US Marshals Service calling cards; over three thousand dollars in cash; and literally hundreds of Western Union dispatches from Sarah, all of which Oliver had read dozens of times.

After carefully placing her latest telegraph into the pouch along with the others, he closed the purse and returned it to his travel bag. A few minutes later, he awakened Mia and the porter arrived to take their lunch orders, creating yet another unforgettable memory for both the marshal and an eloquently dressed young lady crossing the country along the Overland Route of the Transcontinental Railroad.

CHAPTER 9

NATURAL WATERWAYS SUCH as the Carson and Truckee Rivers, as well as the streams and tributaries that flowed into or out of them, were a vital resource for Northern Nevada and California residents. As well as being an essential part of the region's gold and silver mining infrastructure, the Carson River Valley was a food and forage source for miners, prospectors, and their livestock. Accordingly, impeding these waterways by building unauthorized dams or other obstructions to the natural flow of them was illegal.

Although Clifford Kasey's strongarm tactics could temporarily serve to discourage the faint of heart, Donovan Hampton wasn't having it, and had rightfully taken measures to restore the barricaded stream's original path. When he realized just how dubious Clifford Kasey's intentions actually were, he was heading into Virginia City to report the arson incident when he and his family were set upon by the hired gunmen.

Donovan and Beverly Hampton did not appear to be wealthy prospectors, nor had it ever been their intention to become such. Much like Oliver Blackstone, Donovan Hampton's dream had been to own a quaint piece of land for himself and his family. Unlike Oliver, Donovan and Beverly headed west in order to escape the spiraling tensions and expanding population of Boston, where the Civil War had left a still-open wound on the American psyche.

Following Mia's birth, Donovan had worked diligently, panning for, and obtaining enough gold to purchase over a hundred acres of unspoiled land in the Carson River Valley. While most of it was a heavily wooded tangle of wilderness, the regions along the western bank of what he'd named Donovan Creek were a picturesque paradise, with a hidden meadow rising from the lower marshlands and extending up to the edge of the forest in the foothills to the northwest.

What Donovan and Beverly viewed as their quaint little homestead; Clifford Kasey saw with a more materialistic eye. Like the California Gold Rush from 1848 to 1855, he believed the Comstock Lode would eventually fizzle out as well. However, the infrastructure that accompanied them would endure for generations, and the key to lasting wealth, in Kasey's view, was ownership of the land upon which that infrastructure would be built.

Travel time between Reno, Nevada, and Saint Louis, Missouri, had been drastically reduced following the completion of the Transcontinental Railroad. A journey that had previously taken as long as five weeks was now possible to complete in as few as five days. In Clifford Kasey's view, railway travel was indeed the future of American industry and commerce.

With one specific route being surveyed, extending from Salt Lake City, Utah, across Nevada, and into Sacramento, California, he stood to make a fortune from the thousands of acres of land he owned; land that he could lease to railroads, generating profits for him for many years to come. The only obstacle he faced was the hundred acres of land that he did not own.

That land, belonging to Donovan and Beverly Hampton, was pivotal to the railroad company's decision to either cross directly through their northern survey zone or utilize an alternate zone forty miles further south. The southern route, while avoiding a hundred acres of land owned by the Hamptons, would also circumnavigate more than a thousand acres owned by Clifford Kasey.

Unlike the Hamptons, Clifford Kasey had no interest in building a home for his family. He'd never been married or had children, being far too self-absorbed to have sown the seeds of either. His sole interest was in building personal wealth and acquiring financial leverage over others. Once the railroad deal was done, he could return to Chicago without ever looking back, and as long as the resulting capital flowed into his account without interruption, he didn't give a damn about Nevada, or the entire Pacific Northwest for that matter.

For Sheriff Walsh, the entire case seemed to be one confusing, king-sized pile of steaming horse shit. Upon discovering the lengths to which Kasey was willing to go—hiring professional killers to ruthlessly murder his neighbors—he was certain the dispute had to have been over something more substantive than mere water access rights. Clifford Kasey had more than enough land to satisfy whatever unspoken desires he had for it, even though he hadn't developed or built anything noteworthy on any of it. Other than a modest ranch house, an oversized dam, and a useless reservoir with no apparent purpose other than choking off the water supply to the Hamptons, the land was completely undeveloped.

There was no livestock on the property, nor preparations for receiving them, and according to the agents at the Virginia City stockyard, there were no records or receipts indicating any such transactions were pending. Despite having verified the connection between Clifford Kasey and the alleged murderer of Donovan and Beverly Hampton, for the life of him, Sheriff Walsh couldn't find anything that could reasonably be considered as a motive for having them killed.

It had certainly not been a crime of passion or an encounter that had quickly escalated and turned deadly. Clifford Kasey had taken the time to hire professional gunslingers to protect a pointless water reservoir and set fire to a neighbor's property. It was foreseeable that such a confrontation would end up getting someone killed, and Sheriff Walsh was now determined to find out why.

As Oliver's and Mia's train reached further into the territory east of Omaha, Nebraska, the cities surrounding the railroad stations became increasingly crowded; the air quality was notably worse; the friction surrounding the conclusion of the Civil War and the assassination of President Abraham Lincoln was still an unmended tear in the very fabric of the region; and a general sense of anxiety seemed to permeate every aspect of human society.

Surprisingly, for both of them, the closer they got to Boston, the more they missed the wide-open spaces and crisp, clean air of the western frontier. By the time they entered the final leg of their journey, crossing from Ohio into Pennsylvania, the excitement of peering out through the window of their first-class Pullman car had long faded. In fact, the only remaining thrill for either of them was the anticipation of seeing Sarah.

Although Mia knew of her uncle Peter, she'd never actually met him. Her only recollection of hearing his name was from the dispatch her father had received, notifying them that her grandfather had passed away, which had been more than a year ago.

"Are you excited?" asked Oliver, squeezing Mia's hand as the train slowed for their final destination.

"I'm scared," Mia replied. Looking up at Oliver with a sudden sense of panic, she asked, "What if he doesn't like me?"

Smiling reassuringly, Oliver said, "Of course he'll like you, sweetheart. In fact, he's going to love you. "

"Do you really think so?" she asked, hopefully.

"Mia, honey, it is impossible not to love you," Oliver replied, placing his arm around her shoulder, and hugging her as they sat there, looking out the window together.

Mia's apprehension seemed to fade, and as the train stopped, Oliver grabbed the larger of the two travel bags, and Mia took the smaller one containing her brushes, toiletries, and other personal items.

"Here we go," said Oliver, stepping out onto the platform and setting down the travel bags before turning to help Mia down the steps behind him.

Sarah spotted him instantly, and completely abandoning her traditional Bostonian decorum, she lifted the hem of her dress and rushed across the platform, jumping into his arms, and kissing him soulfully. Following their almost indecent public display of affection, they parted with Oliver's large hands still holding her upper arms as he stepped back to drink in the sight of her.

"You are even more beautiful than I remember," he said. "And I thought of you every day," he added with a smile, before hugging her to him again.

"I've missed you with every single heartbeat," Sarah sighed, closing her eyes and exhaling, with her cheek pressed firmly against his chest. When she at last re-opened them, she noticed the young girl near the steps of the railway car, standing demurely with her feet together, and holding her travel case with both satin-gloved hands neatly in front of her.

As if in a trance, Sarah said, "Where are my manners?" Slowly stepping away from Oliver and smoothing the front of her dress with both hands, Sarah smiled and extended one of them towards the little girl. "You must be Mia," she said softly.

"Yes, ma'am," Mia replied, taking Sarah's hand, and saying, "It is very nice to meet you."

"My, oh my! Aren't you the most precious thing ever?" she exclaimed, before saying, "My name is Sarah Hutchins, and the pleasure is all mine."

As Oliver picked up their travel bags, he could only smile as he watched the two of them. Seconds earlier, they had been complete strangers, yet Mia's magical disposition had obviously crossed the continent as well, because Sarah was already undeniably enamored with her.

"Have you seen my uncle?" asked Mia, politely adding, "His name is Peter Hampton."

"I've not yet had the pleasure," said Sarah, looking around the crowded platform as if searching for someone with whom she was actually acquainted. Taking Mia's hand and looping her other arm into Oliver's, she said, "I'm sure he's already here somewhere searching for you, and we'll find him together."

He wasn't, and they didn't.

CHAPTER 10

"WHERE WAS PETER?" seemed to be the question dominating the thoughts of everyone from Oliver and Sarah to Sheriff Walsh back in Virginia City. He'd sent an urgent telegraph attempting to reach Peter Hampton after recovering the bodies of Donovan and Beverly, while Mia was waiting inside the restaurant with Nancy. He'd sent another one after relinquishing custody of Mia to Marshal Blackstone, and had received confirmation from the Western Union telegraph agent that both dispatches had been successfully transmitted and received.

Oliver had also sent two separate dispatches from stops along the route from Reno to Boston, informing Peter of their arrival time. However, he hadn't received a reply, and after following up with the telegraph offices in both Promontory Point, Utah, and Omaha, Nebraska, neither of them was in possession of a dispatch response from Peter Hampton.

While Oliver had no reason to distrust the Western Union agents in Promontory Point or Omaha, he was almost certain that the agent in

Virginia City was serving two masters, one of them being Clifford Kasey. Marshal Blackstone had always had a healthy distrust of Western Union telegraph agents, viewing them as far too susceptible to bribery, blackmail, or coercion. If that proved to be the case with the agent in Virginia City, the reason no one had heard from Peter Hampton was likely because he was already dead.

When Sheriff Walsh showed up at the telegraph office with two deputies in tow, the look on the man's face immediately revealed that Marshal Blackstone's suspicions, at least as they related to the compromised Western Union agent, had been correct. Further investigation revealed that the dispatch intended for Peter Hampton had instead been delivered to a man in Chicago, Illinois, named Victor Graham.

Although an unknown commodity west of the Mississippi River, Victor Graham was a wanted man and a cold-blooded killer, operating between Illinois and the eastern seaboard. He was effective and incredibly dangerous because he appeared to be completely harmless, lulling his victims into a false sense of security before murdering them, often at close range with his weapon of choice, a pearl-handled straight razor.

He'd approached Peter the day following receipt of the telegraph dispatch from Virginia

City, posing as a life insurance claims disbursement officer. Using the official telegraph sent from Sheriff Walsh, he'd easily convinced Peter to welcome him into the formerly lavish family home of his recently deceased father, Alexander Hampton. The Bostonian mansion was in a severe state of disrepair after only one year, with Peter having already squandered the lion's share of his inheritance.

Upon hearing Donovan and Beverly had left everything to him, Peter seemed almost indifferent to the fact that his brother and sister-in-law had just been brutally murdered, and didn't raise a single question regarding the whereabouts of his niece, Mia. He was only too happy to usher the undercover killer into the receiving parlor, where his decaying cadaver was still seated. He was slumped over a stack of blank papers, having bled out over them after his throat had been transected from ear-to-ear. While believing he was about to sign the transfer of ownership of all his brother's worldly possessions, it was actually his own death certificate which had been issued and executed by Victor Graham.

After notifying the local authorities and connecting them with the sheriff in Virginia City, Nevada, Oliver explained to Sarah why he'd been assigned to accompany Mia back to Boston. Before that moment, she'd never even suspected that Oliver had formerly been a federal marshal.

As Mia's legal guardian and an officer of the law, Oliver's instinctive reaction was to move her to a safe location at a hotel where he could personally limit access to her. The visceral reaction that his suggestion elicited from Sarah immediately forced the abandonment of his hastily-devised plan.

"You will do no such thing!" Sarah declared resolutely. "Can't you see the poor girl is exhausted?" The two of you have been running and looking over your shoulders since you left Virginia City, and the last thing she needs is to spend another day... another second worrying about her safety. I'll simply not stand for it!"

Sarah said to the two of them, "Both of you will be staying with me and my father until this matter has been fully resolved. Until such time, you're my personal guests, and you are welcome to stay for as long as you'd like. "

Oliver could tell there was no ambiguity in her resolve. In fact, he was exceedingly impressed with her. During his prolonged absence, she had matured, and the impressionable young lady he'd left behind five years ago was now an intellectually secure woman with a notably steadfast character.

"I want to stay with Sarah," said Mia, looking up at Oliver while tugging rebelliously at his hand.

"It seems you've got me surrounded," said Oliver, smiling as he willingly relented to Sarah's and Mia's demands.

Surprisingly, Sarah's father, Leonard Hutchins, was a changed man upon seeing the US Marshals Service badge adorning Oliver's left lapel, believing as Sarah had that this was a recent development.

"Well, well, Marshal Blackstone, welcome back to the city of Boston," he said, warmly ushering them into the house. "I see the western frontier has left you a changed man," he added, enthusiastically shaking Oliver's hand.

"And who is this little angel?" he asked, bending over, and offering her his hand.

"My name is Mia, and it is very nice to meet you, sir," she said in her customarily polite manner as she kindly accepted his hand.

"Such a delightful child," said Leonard, standing to look at Oliver. "Nothing like the unruly youngsters here in Boston," he added with a smile.

Taking Mia's hand, Sarah said, "Let's get you settled in, shall we? I'm sure you're exhausted after such an exciting day. "

As they passed through the foyer, Mia was utterly speechless. The house was immense, with decorative marble floors, large castle-like doors leading into a number of different rooms, and ornate wooden handrails leading up a staircase lined with elaborate oil paintings mounted inside decorative gold-plated frames. It was unlike anything Mia had ever imagined, dwarfing the opulence of both the first-class Pullman coach and the International Hotel in Virginia City.

Upon reaching and entering the guest room on the second floor, Mia was nearly overwhelmed as she looked around the expansive bedroom chamber. When Sarah asked, "Are you hungry?" all Mia could do was nod in agreement.

Sarah opened the bedroom door and spoke to someone in the hallway, asking, "Layla dear, would you be so kind and bring Mia some soup and biscuits from the kitchen downstairs?"

"Yes, ma'am," came the reply from outside the door, before Sarah closed it again and joined Mia over by the large window, where she was gazing down into the grassy courtyard below.

"How about we get you out of these things and into something a bit more comfortable?" Sarah said, sitting Mia on a chair and unlacing her boots to remove them. "Aren't these adorable?" she noted, honestly admiring them.

"Oliver bought them for me in Virginia City," said Mia. "But I couldn't wear them until we got to Reno."

"Really?" said Sarah, smiling as she slipped them from Mia's feet.

"Yes, ma'am," said Mia. "He bought the dress for me too!" Sliding from the chair, she completed an awkward pirouette before asking, "Isn't it nice?"

"It certainly is," Sarah agreed before unfastening the decorative hooks and eyelets and helping her out of it. After retrieving the nightgown from her travel bag and dressing her in it, Sarah folded the dress and placed it on the bed, saying, "I'll have Layla get this properly cleaned for you tomorrow."

Just at that moment, there was a knock at the door, and a young woman entered carrying a tray with soup and biscuits. The food smelled delicious, but Mia's attention was riveted on the mahogany-skinned woman wearing a sharply-pressed black dress, with a white apron and matching bonnet.

"Layla, dearest, would you mind seeing that this gets cleaned and pressed for Mia tomorrow morning, please?"

"Of course, Miss Sarah," replied the woman, collecting the garment from the bed while eyeing Mia with a glowing smile.

"You're so pretty!" blurted Mia as she stared unblinkingly at her.

"Why, thank you, miss," Layla replied, stopping to nod at the charming young girl before exiting the room.

"My name is Mia, and thank you for the food," she said, as if trying to delay her and steal a final glance at the uniquely exotic woman.

"You're very welcome," Layla replied, slipping out the door and quietly closing it behind her.

While Mia ate her meal, Sarah removed the remaining clothes from her travel bag to place them inside the drawers of a large cedar dresser. Oliver had them all laundered during their stay at the Frontier Hotel prior to departing Reno, and although they were clean, Sarah couldn't help but notice the odd assortment of clothing in her luggage.

"Are all of these for you?" she asked, paying particular attention to the bib overalls, flannel shirt, and clunky brown Brogans.

"Yes, ma'am," said Mia, explaining, "Oliver said I needed to look like a boy, so I wore these on the wagon ride to Reno."

"Why did you need to look like a boy?" asked Sarah, sitting on the edge of the bed across from Mia's dining table near the bedroom window.

"So that the bad men who killed my parents wouldn't recognize me," Mia answered. Chuckling sarcastically, she added, "It didn't really matter though, because they found us anyway, so I could have worn my new dress and boots the whole time."

"Wait a minute... What do you mean, they found you anyway?" Sarah asked, stammering.

"While we were in the wagon, they found us, so Oliver stopped and I hid behind two big rocks and some sagebrush until he came back for me," Mia explained, as if reminiscing about a typical day on the western frontier.

Sarah's heart was racing as she envisioned the drama in her mind. The feeling of suspense she felt was much like that experienced when frontiersmen regaled their captivated listeners with their fanciful tales of the Wild West.

"What happened next?" asked Sarah, nervously clutching the bib overalls tightly in her hands as if anticipating the sound of gunfire.

"Oliver came back and got me," Mia said, leaning back in her chair and kicking her feet gleefully beneath the table after finishing the last of her soup and biscuits. "Then we went to Reno, and I got to wear my new dress and boots."

Looking over at Sarah, Mia asked, "Is it okay if I go to bed now? I'm ever so tired," she said, yawning as her sleepy little eyes began to narrow into drowsy slits.

"Of course," said Sarah, tearing her mind away from Mia's fascinating account with great difficulty and pulling back the covers of the soft, comfortable bed for the tired child.

Upon slipping between the cool sheets, the exhilaration of the day closed in on her, and

Mia began to drift off, saying, "Thank you for everything, Sarah."

"You're welcome, sweetheart," Sarah replied, before kissing Mia's forehead and saying, "Goodnight."

When she started to stand and leave the room, Mia's eyes suddenly sprang open, and she tightly clutched Sarah's hand, asking, "Will you stay with me until after I fall asleep?"

"But of course I will," said Sarah, laying down on top of the covers, facing Mia. Reaching out to brush the hair from the sleepy girl's eyes, she asked, "Mia, honey. What happened to those bad men who were looking for you?"

"Oh, yeah," mumbled Mia, with her eyes slowly falling shut. "Oliver killed them."

"What?" gasped Sarah incredulously, although very quietly, before asking, "All of them?"

"Not all of them," said Mia, in a voice quickly fading. Yawning, she murmured, "He killed the first one in a gunfight... behind the sheriff's office... in Virginia City," she whispered, before finally drifting off to sleep.

CHAPTER 11

THE HUTCHINS MANOR was literally a fortress. Due to the critical role Hutchins Steel played during both the Civil War and the Reconstruction Period, currently in full swing, men like Leonard Hutchins were crucial in helping pull the country back together again. Nevertheless, that national level of engagement came with its downsides.

Due to the number of threats received on a weekly basis, Leonard Hutchins was perpetually under the seamless protection of a veritable army of Pinkerton security agents. The compound surrounding their private estate was accessible only to guests personally escorted into the property by Leonard or Sarah Hutchins, or individuals thoroughly vetted by the Pinkerton Agency, days ahead of their anticipated arrival.

Despite being a personal guest of Sarah and a United States marshal, even Oliver Blackstone's credentials had been thoroughly verified by the Pinkerton Agency within hours of his arrival at the estate. That level of detail suited Oliver just fine, because with his return to active service, the last thing he wanted was for the bounty on his head to endanger his loved ones. At least while inside the residential compound, that would be virtually impossible.

"Mia's asleep," said Sarah. "The poor thing was exhausted."

"It's been a challenging past few days," said Oliver, adding, "But I think we're both glad to finally be here." Thank you for your hospitality, Sarah and Mr. Hutchins. "

"I believe we're beyond the formalities here, Oliver," said Sarah's father. "Call me Leonard, and it's a pleasure to host the two of you."

Looking at Sarah, Leonard said, "Oliver was telling me that he's been with the US Marshals Service now for over fifteen years. I honestly had no idea!"

"Apparently, that was one of the best-kept secrets in Boston," Sarah replied, looking inquisitively at Oliver.

"Well, while based in Texas, I was apparently too good at my job, and that didn't sit well with a large segment of the outlaw population," Oliver explained. "I was placed on an extended, mandatory leave of absence and moved here shortly before meeting Sarah."

"Don't you think that's something that would have been worth mentioning?" asked Sarah, with an admonishing glance.

"I left Texas with an outlaw bounty of nearly one hundred thousand dollars on my head,"

Oliver explained. "I came here to escape my past. I never expected to meet such a delightful young woman as Sarah, and the last thing I wanted was for my past to put our future in danger." Looking at Sarah, he said, "I would never have forgiven myself had anything happened to you."

"So, you were willing to let me believe that you were an opportunistic drifter, rather than just tell me you were a federal marshal... because you were protecting Sarah?"

"I suppose so," said Oliver, looking sheepishly at Sarah. "It seemed the honorable thing to do at the time," he confessed, adding, "Besides, I had a plan."

"And you went all the way to Virginia City, Nevada, to start marshalling again?" asked Leonard. Chuckling aloud, he said, "You could have done that right here in Boston. Lord knows, we could certainly have used a good man like you. "

"He didn't go there as a marshal," said Sarah, smiling. "He went there to build a future for us." Looking at Oliver, she said, "Had he asked me to, I would have gone with him, and never looked back."

"Well, it seems we've all made some ill-considered decisions in the past, but for whatever reasons that brought you back here, you can certainly count on my full-throated support," said Leonard.

"Actually, I came back for Sarah," said Oliver. "I purchased a hundred acres of land over in Springfield, and put some money aside for a house, some horses, and a few head of cattle."

"He asked me to marry him, and I said yes!" interjected Sarah.

Following a brief pause, Leonard extended his hand to Oliver and said, "Then, I suppose congratulations are in order!"

"Thank you, Leonard," said Oliver, accepting and shaking his hand.

"As I recall, the last time you asked for my blessings first," said Leonard, reflectively.

"Like you said, we've all made some ill-considered decisions in the past," Oliver replied, winking at a positively beaming Sarah.

With the impending collapse of his carefully crafted plan, Clifford Kasey was attempting to clean house. The arrest of the Western Union telegraph agent had come within one degree of separation from him. Although he'd supplied the money for the bribe, it had actually been delivered by Blink Masterson, and he would definitely not be implicating anyone.

Having occasionally utilized the services of Victor Graham while residing in Chicago, Kasey knew that setting that killer loose on anyone was a guarantee the problem would be eliminated. The man was as slippery as an eel, and unlike the Washoe Kid, he had no such aversion to murdering children. Once his fee was paid, his customers could rest assured that the job would be done.

While wrapping up his own land-lease deal with the Union Pacific railroad, he assured them there would be no further objections from the owners of the Hampton parcel. Afterwards, he wired the required advance payment into Victor Graham's account, retaining him to handle the Mia Hampton "situation."

Victor was still in Massachusetts, wrapping up some additional "wet" work prior to returning to Chicago, when he received Kasey's dispatch. "How convenient," he said aloud upon reading the message; however, other than the names of Mia Hampton and the marshal accompanying her to Boston, there were no additional details provided.

For Victor Graham, none of that was of concern to him after reading the name Marshal Oliver Blackstone. That was someone he'd been hunting for the past seven years and had never come close enough to even get crosshairs on him. The man was a ghost, avoiding all the pitfalls most lawmen commonly make upon hanging up their badges. They would normally use their credentials to receive preferential treatment or as a reference for future employment. Oliver Blackstone had done none of those things, and after more than five years of frustration, Graham now had at least a reference point as to where he could resume his years-long personal manhunt. For the hundred-thousand-dollar bounty on Blackstone's head, Victor would kill Mia, the marshal, and anyone else who happened to be standing in his way.

Unbeknownst to either Victor Graham or Clifford Kasey, the US Marshals Service had been employing a relatively new investigative technique that they'd adopted from the Pinkerton Detective Agency, known as "following the money." During the course of their investigations into federal crimes, such as assassination conspiracies, they would surreptitiously monitor suspicious funds transfers, especially those involving interstate monetary transactions.

When Blink Masterson deposited cash into the Wells Fargo account of Victor Graham, a man wanted by the US Marshals Service in connection with a number of murder for hire allegations, they were unable to make the connection to his target, Peter Hampton. However, with Clifford Kasey now having made a second deposit, there was unassailable proof of a connection between the two men. Furthermore, having included the names of Mia Hampton and a federal marshal in the deposit memo, there was no doubt as to the assassin's intended targets.

This time, the US Marshals Service acted immediately, advising both Sheriff Walsh, in Virginia City, Nevada, and Marshal Blackstone, in Boston, Massachusetts, of the active termination contract. Although for Sheriff Walsh, the motive behind his actions was still unclear, there could be no further doubt of Clifford Kasey's direct involvement.

    Accordingly, he no longer needed the statements of either Mia Hampton or Charlie Spurlock, and after presenting this new evidence to the US Circuit Court Judge in Virginia City, Nevada, Sheriff Walsh, and deputy Jimmy Pierce immediately headed over to the Kasey ranch with a federally sanctioned warrant for the arrest of Clifford Kasey.

    That same news hit Marshal Oliver Blackstone like a slug to the chest. He'd only been in Boston for two days, and already a hired assassin on the US Marshals Service's "Ten Most Wanted" list was after him and Mia. Despite the joy he felt at being reunited with his bride-to-be, he was under no false impressions regarding who he was or what he did.

    Like Victor Graham, Marshal Oliver Blackstone was a skilled and experienced killer. With very few exceptions, he treated everyone who was anywhere around him with varying degrees of suspicion at all times. His focus could switch from a friend to a foe within a fraction of a second, with the latter never afforded more than a single, fleeting opportunity to execute an attempt on his life. Challenging him face-to-face was something only a handful of now-dead-men had ever dared to do, the last of whom being an unwitting Blink Masterson.

Oliver suspected that a man like Victor Graham had done his homework, and would almost certainly be aware of that, adjusting his tactics accordingly. What Graham didn't know, is that Marshal Oliver Blackstone already knew he was coming for them, and at most, he would only get one shot.

Even had he known, the allure of owning the reputation for being the man who'd taken down Marshal Blackstone was as tempting as a new gold strike to a prospector. However, with a mark like Oliver Blackstone, once he committed to hazarding an assassination attempt, Victor Graham could not afford to miss.

CHAPTER 12

WHEN SHERIFF WALSH and Jimmy Pierce mounted up to leave Virginia City, the deputy noted, "I've never seen you wearing a pistol on your hip before."

"There's a time for everything," replied Sheriff Walsh without further comment.

As a former detective for the Pinkerton Agency, he'd grown accustomed to wearing his service weapon in a holster concealed beneath his jacket. In his view, openly wearing a weapon discouraged normal law-abiding citizens from engaging with him during the course of his daily duties. Today, however, he was unconcerned with Kasey's personal impressions. He was there to arrest a man suspected of ordering the assassinations of a seven-year-old girl, her parents, Donovan and Beverly, her uncle, Peter, and the US marshal Sheriff Walsh had personally appointed as her legal guardian. Frankly, he hoped the son of a bitch would shit himself.

When they arrived at the ranch, there was a flurry of activity underway as Clifford Kasey prepared to leave Nevada. Upon reaching the preliminary agreement with the Union Pacific Railroad, they agreed to finance the security personnel required to protect both the land and the materials that would potentially be staged there once construction was set to begin.

Since there was absolutely nothing there to protect and there were no threats against which protection was required, Clifford Kasey had used the money to hire a handful of second-rate gunslingers rather than the hundreds of men that would normally be required to patrol and protect several thousand acres of leased land.

When the sheriff dismounted his Palomino mare, Deputy Pierce remained seated with the.44 Henry rifle across his saddle, pointed towards the house. A few seconds later, Clifford Kasey walked out onto the porch, accompanied by three armed men, and said, "Sheriff Walsh, to what do I owe the pleasure of this unexpected visit?"

"I have a warrant for your arrest on suspicion of conspiracy to commit murder," answered Sheriff Walsh without flinching.

"I haven't murdered anyone," said Clifford, adding, "Anyone who claims I have is a damned liar!"

"You don't have to pull the trigger to be guilty of conspiracy, and this isn't a request," stated the sheriff. Appraising the other three men on the porch, he said, "Right now, I have a warrant for the arrest of one man: Clifford Kasey. As long as the three of you don't attempt to interfere with the execution of this lawful warrant, you will all be free to go. Otherwise, I'd be happy to arrange sleeping accommodations for you right alongside him in my jailhouse. Oh, and I wouldn't advise doing anything that could make Deputy Pierce start firing rounds from that Henry repeater. I hear that thing leaves a nasty hole. "

Two of the gunmen seemed ready to take their chances, considering the odds were in their favor. Suddenly, the third man said, "To hell with this. I came here to protect railroad property; not to trade gunfire with a sheriff and his deputy." Raising his hands, he stepped away from Kasey and his remaining two gunmen.

"Well, at least we know which of you is the smartest of the three," said Sheriff Walsh.

"He'll be joining you later," said the large, bearded man to the left of a grinning Clifford Kasey. An instant later, he was reaching for his Colt, a split second before the other gunman to Kasey's right grabbed for his.

The impact of a .45 caliber round to the chest at close range tossed the bearded bodyguard back into the wall of the house before the barrel of his pistol could even clear the holster. The second gunshot was much louder as the round from the Henry rifle literally severed the arm of the second gunman above the elbow. His hand was still clutching the grip of his Peacemaker as it lay motionless on the floor of the porch. In a state of shock, the man reached for his arm, tumbling from the porch, and falling face-first into the dirt while bleeding out.

The third man raised his hands even higher, reaffirming his voluntary concession as Deputy Pierce preemptively rotated the barrel of the Henry towards him.

Clifford Kasey's hands were also raised in front of him. He hadn't even attempted to draw on the sheriff, opting instead to piss himself, with a large urine stain appearing on his upper right thigh and rapidly expanding downwards, soiling the expensive riding boot into which his trousers were stylishly tucked.

"You are under arrest for conspiracy to commit multiple murders," said the sheriff, climbing the porch steps to place iron wrist bars on the detainee. Deputy Pierce released one of the horses from the hitching post and guided it to the steps, where Sheriff Walsh helped Kasey into the saddle.

Turning to the last remaining man, the sheriff said, "Son, this life isn't for everyone. If you'll help me load these men's bodies onto their horses, I'll give you a five-minute head start. Deputy Pierce and I are riding into Virginia City. You are free to ride in any other direction, and I would suggest that you head back to wherever it is you rode in from, because if I ever see you in my county again, I will arrest you as an accessory. Are we clear?" asked the sheriff.

"As clear as Lake Tahoe," replied the man, adding, "Which is where I plan to be no later than tomorrow evening."

Once the bodies of the dead men were strapped down securely across the backs of their horses, the anonymous rider mounted his own and headed south. Five minutes later, Sheriff Walsh, Deputy Pierce, and Clifford Kasey were headed west to Virginia City.

When Sheriff Walsh and Deputy Pierce reached the outskirts of town, there was already a small group of young boys there, waiting to see who they had brought in. The normally dismissive Clifford Kasey stared blankly ahead as he was led down Main Street in the direction of the sheriff's office.

By the time they arrived, there was a rather large crowd of curious onlookers gathered outside the jailhouse. That curiosity quickly turned to outrage as a number of disgruntled citizens recognized Clifford Kasey.

"It's about time someone dragged in that thieving son of a jackal!" shouted one angry man, as another screamed, "That's the coyote who foreclosed on my property!"

"I see that the good citizens of Virginia City have eagerly come to your defense," said the sheriff, assisting Clifford Kasey as he dismounted the horse with cuffed wrists. While being led through the angry but peaceful crowd, one prospector spat out a large, sticky brown gob of chewing tobacco, striking the toe of Clifford's brushed suede riding boot.

Turning sharply towards the antagonist, he said, "Sheriff, that man just assaulted me!"

"Now the outside matches the inside," said the sheriff under his breath, as he marched Kasey up the steps and into the jailhouse without missing a beat.

"When this is over, I will have your badge," spat Kasey, venomously. "My attorneys will eviscerate you for the treatment I've received while in your custody, and I will most certainly have the final word in this matter!"

"But, you'll have it in court, before a jury of your peers," said Sheriff Walsh. "That's a hell of a lot more than Donovan and Beverly Hampton ever got," he added, guiding Clifford Kasey through the heavy iron security door and into a holding cell near the back of the jailhouse.

After locking him inside, he said, "Place your hands through the opening please," motioning towards the serving slot through which his meal trays would be inserted. While removing the iron wrist bars, he said, "Tomorrow morning, you'll be taken into custody by United States marshals, so please feel free to enjoy our luxurious accommodations until that time."

As he turned and left the holding cell area, Fred Walsh completely ignored the stream of hollow threats and unbecoming obscenities echoing down the narrow hallway from behind him. Closing the iron security door, he said, "Donovan. Beverly. We're finally going to get you some justice. "

Jimmy Pierce and another deputy were outside the jailhouse, making sure the rapidly-growing crowd gathering in front of the steps remained peaceable and did not escalate into a lynch-mob. Clifford Kasey had made a lot of enemies in Virginia City after having purchased a number of title loans and immediately foreclosed on the properties the instant their monthly mortgage payments were overdue.

Using the deceptive banking techniques he'd developed and perfected in Chicago, Illinois, he made certain that upon transfer of the loan notes to him, they were already a minimum of fourteen days delinquent. Then, without any additional legal notice required, he would demand payment in full. When the borrowers couldn't pay, he immediately seized their property and forcibly evicted them from their land.

Despite the obvious unethical aspect of his behavior, there was nothing illegal about it, and it had allowed him to subversively confiscate thousands of acres of land along the Carson River Valley. When he encountered the obstacle presented by Donovan and Beverly Hampton, his wildly successful technique didn't work, because there was no loan note to purchase.

As newly-seeded migrants from Boston, they were unable to get a bank loan, so Donovan always paid cash for everything. After several years of industrious work, the Hamptons were absolutely self-sufficient, with Donovan only seldom venturing into Virginia City for supplies and items he and Beverly couldn't hunt, grow, or make for themselves.

The only conceivable way to get them off of their land was to either choke off their water supply or burn them out of it. When neither of those attempts succeeded, Kasey had them killed.

While this was currently only a developing theory in the mind of Sheriff Walsh, the evidence of its probability was currently gathered neatly out in front of his office. Although it still wasn't a satisfactory motive for the unsolved puzzle in his mind, it was a dangling thread at which he would continue to tug.

For the remainder of the day, deputies Pierce and Haywood alternated their watch of the high-profile detainee. As evening drew near, the assembled crowd of curious sensation-seekers began to dwindle, and by nightfall, only Deputy Pierce remained seated in a chair under the overhang outside the jailhouse.

"It's been a long day," said Sheriff Walsh, approaching from down the wooden sidewalk to relieve his deputy and assume protective custody of their prisoner until morning.

"It certainly has," replied Jimmy, standing to greet the approaching sheriff. "I never realized just how many folks had a bone to pick with Clifford Kasey, and for a while there, I thought we were about to have a riot on our hands," said the smiling deputy.

"Well, I have full confidence in your ability to placate a peaceful gathering of law-abiding townsfolk," said the sheriff, nodding reverently. "I was proud of the way you handled yourself out at the ranch this morning." "Outstanding work," Sheriff Walsh added.

"Thank you, sheriff," Jimmy replied, grinning, and tipping his hat back on his head. "I have to say, I never knew you were so handy with a six-gun," he stated in obvious admiration.

"Like I said this morning," replied the sheriff. "There's a time for everything."

"Apparently so," said Jimmy, adding, "And right now, it's time for me to hit the hay, because morning comes early in Virginia City."

"Goodnight, Jimmy," said Sheriff Walsh as the deputy headed down the walkway and disappeared into an adjoining alley. Stepping inside, he poured himself a cup of piping hot coffee from the fresh pot on top of the potbelly stove, and settled in for a long evening.

It was nearly midnight when he heard a single horse approaching from down the otherwise empty street. After walking over and peering through the window next to the front door, he grabbed his rifle and stepped out onto the porch, into the shadow under the overhang.

There was a beautiful black mare tied to the hitching post in front of the hardware store next door. The moonlight overhead reflected faintly from the dazzling array of silver studs adorning the horse's saddle and saddlebags, and Charlie Spurlock was walking slowly towards him.

"Stop right there," stated the sheriff, leveling the Henry repeater directly on Spurlock and saying, "That's as far as you go."

Spurlock said nothing, and two shots rang out simultaneously as the sheriff's body twisted, falling from the porch and onto the ground below. As he lay there, struggling to remain conscious, another shot rang out from inside the jailhouse, followed by the sound of footsteps walking down the wooden planks of the sidewalk, and the sound of a horse's hooves digging briskly into the dusty street, before fading into the distant darkness that slowly enshrouded everything.

CHAPTER 13

WHEN DEPUTY HAYWOOD heard the gunshots, he bolted upright in his bed and ran out of the bunkhouse in his stocking feet, with his Peacekeeper in hand, and wearing only long johns. When he spotted the sheriff's body on the ground near the porch, he broke into a full sprint, yelling for help at the top of his lungs. On the porch, he frantically rang the alarm bell before jumping down to the ground and kneeling beside the sheriff.

"He's alive! Someone go wake up the doctor and get him over here!" shouted Deputy Haywood, as Jimmy and two other deputies came running down the street in various stages of dress, but all armed to the teeth.

Running inside the building, Jimmy noticed the security door was open, and Kasey's jail cell was still shut, but their normally talkative guest was suspiciously silent. Peering into the cell, he saw that what wasn't still attached to the leftovers dangling from the busted melon atop Clifford Kasey's neck was spattered against and slowly dripping down the bricks lining the back wall.

"God Almighty!" he exclaimed, dashing back outside, and saying, "They got to Kasey!"

Running over to the edge of the porch, Jimmy saw that Sheriff Walsh was in bad shape, but he was still alive. "Hang in there sheriff. Help is on the way," he said comfortingly as deputy Haywood rested Walsh's head on the leg placed gently beneath the nape of his neck.

Through the fog of the searing pain burning in the left side of his chest, Sheriff Walsh gasped, "It was Spurlock," before coughing up a mouthful of blood that trickled down the sides of his face.

Finally, Doctor Spencer arrived, carefully turning the sheriff onto his right side to remove the jacket covering his wound. To everyone's surprise, there was no blood.

The bullet had smashed into the holstered service revolver, concealed beneath the sheriff's coat. The impact had fractured several ribs, with one of them puncturing his lung. He was in a tremendous amount of pain, but Doctor Spencer was determined that the resulting injury would not be a fatal one.

After carefully rolling him onto a gurney, several deputies and other concerned citizens helped carry the sheriff down the sidewalk to Doctor Spencer's office, where they took him inside and placed him on an elevated wooden surgery table. The doctor went to work on him right away, and after several tense hours, he finally emerged, saying, "Sheriff Walsh is going to feel that one for several weeks, but he should be back on his feet in no time." Looking around at the cadre of relieved deputies who had been standing watch while the doctor operated on him, Spencer said, "We can probably consider ourselves blessed to have the luckiest sheriff in the history of Virginia City."

Marshal Blackstone received word from the US Marshals Service field office in Virginia City, Nevada, relaying both the news of the apprehension of Clifford Kasey and the report of his murder, along with the near-fatal shooting of Sheriff Walsh. By that time, law enforcement officials had already determined the identity of the alleged shooter as Charlie Spurlock. However, no one other than Mia or Clifford Kasey would have been able to tie him to the murders of Donovan and Beverly Hampton.

Spurlock honestly believed he'd finally tied up nearly every remaining loose end, but yet again, he'd ridden off into the night without making sure the job was actually done. He'd now, having unsuccessfully attempted to murder a sheriff during the process of executing a detainee in protective custody, further aggravated a problem he formerly viewed as a fading memory.

Although Sheriff Walsh had issued a sworn statement stating that Charlie Spurlock was the shooter, he would still need to testify and identify Spurlock in court for those charges to stand. This left Spurlock an opportunity, albeit a narrow one, to clean up this lingering mess and walk away without feeling a noose around his neck.

Before murdering the Hamptons, Charlie Spurlock had already killed several men. Most of them had been gunslingers much like himself, hoping to secure a place in history as being among the fastest guns in the west. As the Washoe Kid, he'd sliced through them like a sickle through straw, incrementally expanding his reputation among rivals as a notoriously deadly adversary.

Sheriff Walsh had expected as much, and knew the only way to confront him was with a weapon drawn down on him, the hammer cocked, and his finger already on the trigger. Still, the speed with which Spurlock had drawn and fired that sidearm was almost inconceivable. He'd barely even seen the man move before he was falling backwards and firing into the sky. Only his customary habit of concealing his weapon for the sake of common courtesy had prevented that slug from popping his heart like a soap bubble.

One thing was certain. The next time he went after Spurlock, it would be with a posse and a duly-issued shoot to kill order.

In Boston, Oliver was somewhat outraged at the news. However, after having targeted a widely respected sheriff and missing, there would be nowhere left for Spurlock to hide. He would be hunted like a rabid bear, and every lawman in the surrounding regions would have a noose on layaway for him.

Still, that didn't put an end to either his or Mia's problems. Even with Kasey dead, the termination fee had already been paid, and a man like Victor Graham would feel ethically obligated to complete the job for which he had been retained.

With the exception of his periodic, unscheduled, and irregularly arranged meetings with his liaison at the local US Marshals Service field office, Oliver rarely left the Hutchins estate. Mia could occupy herself with plenty of activities inside the secure five-acre compound, and there, he could look after her until Victor Graham had been apprehended.

Each morning, Sarah departed with a protective detail of Pinkerton agents, who escorted her to and from the elementary school where she worked. When she returned, she and Mia would go over those very same lessons together, during which time Sarah discovered that Mia was already a very advanced student.

"Who taught you to read so well?" asked Sarah, seriously intrigued.

"My mom would read to me every night when I was a little girl, and when I was five, I could read some things too," Mia explained.

"What are some of your favorite stories?" asked Sarah.

"I love the stories by *Peter Parley* because they are about far-away places," said Mia, adding, "But my favorite story is about a princess whom everyone made special things for because they wanted to marry her, but in the end, she married the man who didn't have anything, because he was the one who really, really loved her."

Sarah was shocked! *Peter Parley* was the pseudonym of *Samuel Griswold Goodrich*, one of her own personal favorite American authors. Furthermore, the story she had just described seemed to be from a recently published book by a Danish author named *Hans Christian Andersen*, called *The Most Incredible Thing*.

"Your mother must have been quite a fascinating woman," said Sarah, fondly.

"She said it was important to read and write because only people who can read and write can make a difference," said Mia, as if recalling something of absolute importance.

"She was right," said Sarah, adding, "And one day, you will be someone who makes a difference."

Mia seemed pleased with Sarah's reassurances and sat there silently for a moment, as if in deep introspection, before saying, "Oliver is like the man from the story."

"And which man would that be?" asked Sarah, smiling.

"The man who wanted to marry the princess, but he didn't have anything to give her," said Mia, explaining, "Oliver told me that he loves you more than anything and wants to take care of you, but that you need things like a house and a quiet piece of land in the countryside, where you can raise a family, and maybe even some horses and a milk cow like Mae."

Looking imploringly into Sarah's eyes, Mia said, "You already have all of those things here, so why did you let him go all the way to Nevada alone, when your father didn't want to marry him anyway?"

Suddenly, there were tears pooling in Sarah's eyes, and her lips started to tremble. She turned to look out the window. She attempted to hide them from Mia, but the observant child had already seen them and said, "I'm sorry, Sarah." I didn't mean to make you cry.

Mia felt terrible and began to cry as well. Turning back towards her, Sarah saw the uncertainty in Mia's eyes and said, "No Mia." You did not say anything wrong, and I'm not crying because of what you said. I'm crying because of what I didn't say. "

The two of them sat staring at each other, not even bothering to hide their tears anymore, and Sarah said, "Five years ago, I let the man I love more than life itself walk out that door without saying anything to stop him, and it took you, Mia, to make me realize how foolish I was."

"Really?" asked Mia, smiling at Sarah through her tears. "So, you're not mad at me?" she queried softly.

"Heavens no!" said Sarah, wrapping her arms tightly around the beloved child as the two of them openly wept together.

"I miss my mom and dad," Mia whispered.

CHAPTER 14

OLIVER WAS INHERENTLY suspicious of anything that broke what he felt to be the daily routine within the environment around him. It wasn't that he expected everything to proceed each day as it had on the previous one; however, changes to trivial details such as the time at which the morning paper was delivered to the watchmen at the compound entrance, the faces of the security agents rotating shifts throughout the week, and the number of visitors in and around the Old North Church near the Hutchins estate, never escaped his scrutiny.

Most of these things were easily observable from his guestroom on the third floor, and despite the excellent service provided by the Pinkerton agents, Oliver never let his own guard down.

During the day, when Sarah was at work, Mia would shadow Layla almost incessantly. The two of them had developed a close relationship over the past several weeks, and after she'd allowed Mia to help her make the morning biscuit dough for the first time, she'd become Layla's constant companion.

Even so, Mia had been cooped up inside the estate for weeks, and longed to venture beyond the high walls of the palatial compound. After reassuring Oliver that she would be under constant protection, Sarah convinced him it would be safe for Mia to go to school with her.

Mia loved it. She was astoundingly smart, exceedingly attentive, and incredibly well-liked by the other children. After her very first day in the classroom, even the engagement of the other children increased dramatically, inspired by the ceaseless hunger for knowledge displayed by their intriguing new classmate. Since all of Sarah's students were the children of politicians, diplomats, or other successful entrepreneurs, they were all accustomed to some type of dedicated personal security, making their learning environment an uncommonly safe one.

Each afternoon, the learning experience would continue as Sarah and Mia would review the lessons of the day together at Mia's insistence. They would re-read stories they had read in the classroom, discuss basic science such as birds, animals, and insects, and indulge Mia's almost insatiable obsession with numbers and arithmetic.

Since Sarah's daily routine outside the estate was almost the absence of a daily routine, it was incredibly difficult to notice a pattern in the tactics of her protection squad. As a result, someone with an obsession for details and an abundance of time, such as Victor Graham, would be required to even begin to decipher the illogic behind her movements.

Rather than attempting to break the code all at once, he'd done so incrementally by using seemingly unrelated factors. Since Sarah never left the estate at the same time on any given day, he began by noting the time of her arrival at the school, which was nearly the same each morning. There were a number of possible routes and combinations thereof that would prevent an average stalker from guessing the prospective paths of Sarah's daily commute, but Victor Graham was not an average stalker.

The arrival time was important because, were she to arrive even a few minutes later than planned, the protection detail at the school would become suspicious and send someone to investigate the delay. This meant that regardless of the departure time from the compound, the arrival time at the school always had to be nearly identical.

Following several weeks of mapping and clocking the various circuitous roadways and bypasses, he concluded his research by noting the daily departure times of Sarah's carriage. By using the charts and maps he'd previously created, he could now successfully narrow the more than two dozen possible route alternatives down to only one or two.

With Oliver Blackstone now officially an active US marshal, it hadn't taken Graham long to discover the location where he and Mia had been sequestered. Nevertheless, he quickly discovered that getting inside that stronghold would be out of the question.

He'd attempted infiltrating the Pinkerton Agency in order to get assigned to the estate protection task force; however, their extensive vetting process could take over a year, and within days they had discovered irregularities in his application, resulting in his permanent disqualification for employment with them. Imitating a Pinkerton agent and attempting to enter the compound during a shift change would require inside knowledge pertaining to the details of their erratic personnel exchanges. Otherwise, merely appearing there unannounced would surely earn him a bullet to the head.

Although Victor Graham had spent weeks cracking Sarah's transportation code, he'd almost convinced himself of its uselessness when he spotted Mia Hampton peeking out from beneath the normally lowered shades of the carriage. With the carriage itself being the equivalent of a Wells Fargo armored gold transport wagon, and with the window shades almost always drawn, taking them out with a long rifle would be impossible. He would have to get close enough to ensure a clean kill without getting caught and eliminated on the spot by her protection detail.

"Hmmm," he thought to himself. *"Now, there's a challenge worthy of my skills."*

A few days later, he finally noticed an opening that would allow him an ever-so-slim window of opportunity. The only individuals who were allowed to proceed past the dual armed guards posted at the entrance of the schoolyard were the private security personnel and coach drivers for the other children in Sarah's classroom. While getting through Sarah's protective detail would have been as difficult as accosting the Queen of England, some of the other bodyguards weren't as meticulous in their duties, and upon exiting the gate on Friday afternoon following school, one of them coughed.

On Sunday evening, he was dead, and a dapper new gentleman with a handlebar moustache and excellent, expertly-forged credentials, reported for duty the following Monday morning to transport the child of a Boston & Albany Railroad executive to school.

Posing as a veteran Wells Fargo transportation security officer named Vincent Wellington, his credentials were only hastily perused before loading a drowsy Theodore Watson into the carriage for a twenty-minute commute across Boston. Along the way, a bottle of chloroform was administered to the sleeping boy to ensure his slumber would last until the carriage had reached the entrance to the schoolyard.

Once there, being a new security escort, he would dismount the carriage to present his credentials to the guards at the gate, quietly dispatching them into the hereafter with his weapon of choice. Then, he could walk right into that classroom and butcher everyone in sight. If having both his beloved Sarah and his protected charge, Mia, slaughtered in a classroom full of children wouldn't force the marshal to finally make a mistake, nothing would.

He was mentally estimating the amount of time he would need to complete his macabre mission when he arrived at the gates of the schoolyard to discover an unexpected surprise: Marshal Oliver Blackstone.

Although Oliver knew that he and Mia were being hunted by Victor Graham, he had no idea what the man looked like. No one did. Victor Graham was a wraith known only by his banking information, his modus operandi, and the trail of human carnage he left in his wake.

For weeks, Oliver had been scanning the area surrounding the compound from his room on the third floor. Just as he had done from the loft in Aunt Karen's house across the street from the International Hotel in Virginia City, he realized that the best place to observe a location is from a different location that no one would ever suspect. Due to the historic relevance of the Old North Church, it wasn't unusual for groups of tourists to visit the tower made famous by Paul Revere's two lighted lanterns. What was unusual was when one single visitor climbed into that very same tower every single school day for over a month.

He may have looked like an introverted American history professor, but he wasn't watching the horizon for an invasion by British naval forces. He was watching the entrance of the Hutchins estate, and when Oliver realized the man was observing the coach transporting Sarah and Mia, even in the absence of a clear and present threat, he began following him.

The curious man was as innocuous as a squirrel, wandering through nearby streets and byways, jotting down notes and calculating travel times and distances by obsessively viewing his ornate pocket watch. None of these things were threatening in or of themselves; however, when he showed up across the park from Sarah's school, where he and Sarah had enjoyed their first picnic together, every alarm in Oliver's gut began to sound.

He left several minutes before Sarah and Mia departed, following a coach driver who was obviously feeling quite unwell, and continued following him to the security firm where he returned the carriage after dropping off one of Sarah's pupils at their home.

Again, there was nothing overly dubious about any of this, but it was a disruption to the flow of the natural timestream in Oliver's reckoning. People have things to do every day. They work, they go to school, they take care of their families, and occasionally, they tie one on and stagger home to a nagging wife at midnight on Friday, following a tough week. This man did none of those things. Even beyond his obsession with taking notes, he just seemed odd and out of place.

That's when Oliver realized how Victor Graham was able to get so close to his targets without alarming them. This unostentatious fellow was probably the mastermind behind the strategies Victor Graham later used to slay his victims.

It was so ingenious, because no one, not even Oliver, would suspect such an insignificant flea of a man of working with a cold-blooded killer like Victor Graham. For the moment, it was only a working theory, but somehow, Oliver's gut told him that an attack on Sarah and Mia at the school was imminent.

That morning, Oliver didn't shadow the flea. Instead, he followed Sarah's coach from a distance, hoping to catch the coyote hosting that flea. When nothing unusual happened along their circuitous Pinkerton-planned route, Oliver was stumped. The guards at the gate behind him had already been alerted and instructed not to abandon their posts under any circumstances. Despite the calm around them, Oliver was certain there was danger in the air, and rarely had his intuition misled him.

When the suspected accomplice showed up driving a security firm carriage with the boy the former driver had dropped off the preceding Friday, Oliver knew his intuition had been spot on. He immediately thought to himself, *"This is a diversionary tactic."*

Neither Victor Graham nor Marshal Blackstone revealed their cards in this deadly game of poker outside the gates of Sarah's school. When the carriage reached and stopped on the short gravel path leading up to the gate, the two men both eyed each other cautiously.

Marshal Blackstone realized that this man was the key to taking down Victor Graham, and Victor Graham saw a one-hundred-thousand-dollar payday, and an enduring place in outlaw history, standing right there in front of him.

"Would you mind stepping down from the carriage, sir?" asked Oliver, eyeing him suspiciously, with the hand above his Colt at the ready.

"Not at all," replied Graham in an almost grovelingly humble manner. After looping the reins over a hook near the coach brake lever, he slowly climbed down and turned to face the marshal, about ten paces away.

"Do you have any weapons other than your sidearm, sir?"

"Only my disarming nature," said the man, attempting to elicit a smile from the stoic marshal.

"And would you mind opening up your jacket and turning around slowly for me?" Oliver asked, again without objection from Graham. The sidearm was securely latched into the holster, presenting no danger to the marshal, and after completing a full rotation, Oliver said, "Thank you sir," motioning for him to relax.

"Is there a problem, marshal?" asked Graham, with a perplexed look on his face.

Oliver still had no reasonable grounds to suspect the man and said, "Just being cautious," before asking, "Do you mind if I see your service credentials?"

Graham was already viewing the deadly choreography in his mind's eye. Once he was close enough, he would be able to kill Oliver quickly, then draw his sidearm and shoot the two dismissive guards behind him, clearly irritated by the marshal's unwarranted interference. Then, he could simply traipse into the building and earn the remainder of his bounty by finishing off Mia and any other unfortunate witnesses and loose ends.

Stepping closer to Oliver, Graham slowly reached into the inner pocket of his jacket. After removing his forged credentials, he lowered his left arm, allowing the straight razor to drop from his sleeve into his palm while extending the papers in his right hand towards the marshal.

The moment Oliver's hand touched the documents, Victor Graham's deadly ballet began. With viper-like speed, he raised the straight razor, flipping it open during the quarter-second long journey from his left side towards Oliver's right jugular. Oliver caught only a glimpse of the gleaming blade before it began its deadly descent, inches from his neck.

Raising his right hand, almost too late, he was able to alter the path of the finely-honed, edged instrument only slightly. Missing the intended mark by a mere two inches, the razor sliced into the right side of Oliver's face as he pivoted, leaving a four-inch, thin red line from the edge of his cheek to the corner of his mouth.

Graham's skillfully-rehearsed, artistic figure-eight arc was prematurely interrupted when the .41 caliber bullet from the Derringer in Oliver's left hand entered below Victor's right eye and blew a four-inch plate of occipital bone through the back of his head. He died with a look of utter and complete shock on his mutilated face, as his spirit danced on, in a body far removed from the one now lying face down in the dirt at Oliver's feet.

CHAPTER 15

THE THIN CUT across Oliver's face was deceiving. The razor had sliced through the outer layers of skin and muscle tissue, actually scraping the cheekbone before terminating slightly to the right of his nose. When the flap of skin opened, the copious amount of blood that poured from it was shocking.

Pulling a handkerchief from his pocket, Oliver folded it together and pressed it tightly against his face, applying as much pressure as possible. One of the security guards from the gate rushed over to him, asking, "How can we help, marshal?"

"Make sure the boy in the back of that carriage is all right, and that no one gets past this gate before I return with backup," said Marshal Blackstone, swinging up into the saddle of his bay horse and taking off in a dead run.

It only took a few minutes for the marshal to reach the field office, co-located inside the precinct building of the Boston Police Department. Within a quarter of an hour, the schoolyard was literally crawling with deputies from the US Marshals Service and Boston police officers. However, Marshal Oliver Blackstone was not one of them.

The laceration to the marshal's face, although no longer life-threatening, did require immediate medical attention. Surprisingly, the extreme sharpness of the razor and the passionate care with which Victor Graham handled that precisely-honed instrument of death resulted in an exceptionally clean incision, comparable to that of a surgeon's scalpel.

Nevertheless, had Oliver not had the foresight to keep constant pressure on the wound, he could easily have bled to death before even reaching the police station. Fortunately, the physician on duty at the precinct was able to clean and disinfect the wound, and after applying a number of surgical sutures, both inside Oliver's mouth and along the exterior four-inch gash, he was able to successfully seal the cut and stem the bleeding.

The procedure had taken nearly two hours while Marshal Blackstone dozed beneath the cloud of an ether-induced slumber. When he regained consciousness several hours later, he discovered the injury had been dressed, and his head was tightly bandaged in a manner that prevented him from speaking normally, chewing, or even yawning.

Initially, neither Sarah nor any of her students inside the classroom were even aware of the deadly confrontation that had just taken place outside the gate. Sarah and the children reacted only when police officers began pouring into the school yard.

Like a mother goose, she quickly wrangled her gaggle of wide-eyed goslings away from the windows and into the far back corner of the classroom, before bolting the door from inside. Within seconds, there was a knock on that same door, accompanied by the familiar voice of one of the security guards.

"Miss Hutchins, this is Clive Baxter," he said calmly.

"Yes, Mister Baxter. Is everything all right?" Sarah asked nervously through the door.

"Yes, ma'am," answered Clive, explaining, "We've just had an attempted security breach." No one here is in any danger, but we'd like you to all remain inside the classroom until the police have cleared the area. "

"Thank you, Mister Baxter," said Sarah, with an obvious sense of relief. "We will all wait here until we hear from you."

"Yes, ma'am," said Clive, adding, "It shouldn't take too long, so please be patient and remain calm."

Within half an hour, every inch of the school grounds and the surrounding property had been searched; every leaf had been overturned; every bystander within a hundred yards of the school had been interviewed; and the body outside the gate had been removed. Immediately thereafter, Sarah was notified and unbolted the door, as anxious as her students were to discover the reason for the unexpected tumult.

Outside, Theodore Watson had literally missed the entire drama, and after having been carried to and secured inside the small guardhouse just beyond the entry gate, he'd continued sleeping until only moments before Sarah released the other children.

"What happened, Teddy?" shouted one of the two young boys, excitedly rushing across the gravel driveway towards him.

"I don't really remember much of anything," said Theodore. "A new coach driver picked me up this morning, and on the way here, we stopped, and he held a smelly rag across my face. I think I passed out after that."

"Wow," said Mike Doherty. "He was probably trying to shanghai you!"

"Yeah," agreed Phillip Rowe, adding, "A lot of people have been shanghaied lately! You're lucky you didn't wake up on a boat headed for China!"

"Hey, everybody!" shouted Mike, turning and rushing towards the other children. "Teddy almost got shanghaied!" he added in wide-eyed amazement.

"They almost took him to China!" added Phillip, turning to follow Mike, and leaving a still-bewildered Theodore standing there by himself to wonder what had even happened.

Despite the absence of official statements by the police confirming any such events had transpired, the "shanghai" story became the prevailing narrative among the children. By the time their respective carriage drivers and security details arrived to collect them, it was all any of them could talk about. Not surprisingly, the sensational rumor continued to spread, quickly traveling home to the children's families and then to the families of other Bostonians. However, it would be days before the story actually appeared in Boston's newspaper headlines.

When Sarah and Mia arrived at home, they were somewhat disappointed when Oliver wasn't there to hear about their dramatic school day. When he hadn't returned by late afternoon, they began to worry, and as nightfall approached, both Sarah and Mia were close to losing their minds. Oliver was never absent for more than an hour whenever they were at home, and with an assassin actively searching for Mia, those absences were very rare occurrences.

When a wagon came through the compound gates, both Sarah and Mia were sitting outside on the front porch. At first, neither of them recognized the passenger seated beside the deputy marshal holding the reins. Once Mia noticed the large reddish-brown, black-stockinged bay horse tied to the back of the wagon, she sprang from her chair as if she'd been stung by a scorpion.

"Oliver!" she screamed, running down the porch steps and across the lawn as fast as her legs could carry her.

Upon hearing Mia call out Oliver's name, Sarah quickly followed, and the two of them rushed towards the wagon, arriving at the edge of the yard just as it came to a stop.

Although still groggy from the somewhat imprecise application of the ether during his surgery, Oliver attempted to climb down the steps of the wagon, missing the final one and tumbling backwards into the lush green lawn. Mia and Sarah also immediately dropped to the ground, with both of them nearly falling on top of him.

Without a word, Oliver opened his arms, taking the two of them into his embrace and hugging them tightly. Layla and the deputy marshal had also rushed over, and they were both standing there, confused, and ready to assist, but after well over a minute with neither of the three in an apparent hurry to move, Layla waved away the deputy and went back up to the porch, taking a seat herself to wait for them.

After releasing the bay stallion and tying him to the hitching post, the deputy said, "Goodnight, Marshal Blackstone," before waving and heading back down the lane towards the gate.

Oliver lifted his right hand for only a moment to wave at the departing deputy, before returning it to Mia's shoulders. Finally, he parted his lips slightly to whisper, "It's over."

The three of them lay there in the thick grass for long enough to actually pique Leonard's curiosity. The sun had just vanished behind the trees when he came outside onto the porch and took a seat in the chair next to Layla.

"Do you have any idea what's going on over there?" asked Mister Hutchins.

"No, sir," Layla replied, shaking her head with a smile, and adding, "But, if ever there were three people on God's green Earth who really loved each other, then we... are looking at them."

Fireflies had already begun their nightly bioluminescent light show when Sarah and Mia finally helped Oliver to his feet and guided him across the lawn and up the steps of the front porch.

Once seated inside the house at the dining table, Layla brought Oliver a bowl of warm broth, strained from the delicious chicken stew the rest of them had eaten earlier. Barely able to open his mouth at all, there were no complaints issuing from it as he finished two full servings before nodding gratefully at Layla.

Normally, Oliver and Sarah would both tuck Mia into bed before adjourning to the sitting room or the front porch to discuss the topics of the day. That night, it was Sarah and Mia who helped Oliver to bed, and after receiving goodnight kisses from both of them, whether from being freed of the daunting specter of Victor Graham, or from the after-effects of the anesthesia, Marshal Oliver Blackstone did something he hadn't done for months. He slept peacefully.

CHAPTER 16

FOR THE FIRST time in many years, Oliver felt truly unencumbered. With Mia no longer in danger and there being no known threats against him, he could seriously consider hanging up his marshal's badge for good and settling down.

The cut on his face healed remarkably quickly, and within two weeks, he was able to start eating solid food again. Although his first attempt at a porterhouse steak proved to be an overly ambitious endeavor, Mia's very own rolled biscuits with fresh butter and sorghum molasses, and Layla's soft scrambled eggs with crispy bacon, seemed to Oliver like a breakfast fit for a king.

A week later, Oliver invited Sarah and Mia on a train trip to Springfield, Massachusetts. It had been years since he'd purchased the property there, and Oliver was anxious to finally survey it for himself.

With their departure from the greater Boston area and the associated, widespread influence of the industrial revolution and post-

Civil War reconstruction projects, the world around them somehow seemed different.

There was a notable change in both the surrounding scenery and the cultural lifestyle of the people living there. Once they arrived in Springfield, Oliver hired a horse and buggy, and the three of them rode out to view the property. It was magnificent.

The parcel stretched along the eastern bank of the Connecticut River, about two miles north of the Massachusetts-Connecticut state line. It consisted of sixty acres of meadowland bordering another forty acres of densely wooded forest, with a bluff overlooking the river where Oliver envisioned building their future home. It was there on that very bluff, surrounded by a stand of eastern white pine trees, that Oliver properly proposed to Sarah.

He presented Sarah with an engagement ring, forged from the same gold ore he'd brought with him, mined from his very own property near Virginia City, Nevada, and crowned with a beautiful princess-cut diamond. Of course, she accepted, and after sealing their official engagement with a long-awaited kiss, both Oliver and Sarah turned to look at Mia.

They'd first spoken about adopting Mia shortly after Oliver arrived with her in Boston and discovered her uncle had been murdered. Neither Oliver nor Sarah could bear the thought of Mia becoming an orphan, but once he'd seen the two of them together on that railroad platform for the first time, Oliver realized just how much he loved them both.

As they stood there, hand in hand, gazing adoringly at the expectant young girl, Oliver said, "Mia, you must know how much we both love you, and even though we can never replace your mom and dad..."

"I'll marry both of you!" exclaimed Mia, gleefully rushing over to hug Sarah and Oliver.

When they parted, Oliver presented Mia with a silver necklace bearing a heart-shaped pendant, fashioned from the same gold as Sarah's ring. It was engraved with the words "Donovan & Beverly" on one side and "Oliver & Sarah" on the other.

"This is to remind you that your parents are always watching over you from Heaven, and Sarah and I will always watch over you from here," said Oliver.

After Sarah affixed the delicate silver chain around her neck, Mia turned to face both of them and said, "This really is the most incredible thing!"

With the sun sinking lower in the afternoon sky, the three of them enjoyed another few minutes, drinking in the indescribable beauty of both the location and the moment. Afterwards, they reluctantly climbed aboard the buggy, nudging the chestnut mare back in the direction of Springfield proper.

They would remain in Springfield overnight, with Mia and Sarah giggling in their hotel room late into the evening. There were wedding plans to be made, guest lists to be created, and a myriad of other details to be considered and arranged. Nevertheless, Sarah and Mia were ecstatic, and Oliver had never been happier.

Upon returning to the Hutchins estate in Boston the following afternoon, Leonard was overjoyed at the news of Sarah's and Oliver's official engagement. The beautiful ring on Sarah's finger was more than substantial proof of Oliver's most honorable intentions, and if his actions had taught Leonard anything, it was that she would be as safe with him as she was within the walls of their current residential sanctuary.

"We're also formally adopting Mia," said Sarah, standing behind the smiling girl with her arms draped over Mia's shoulders.

At first, it appeared as if Leonard was going to sneeze, because he quickly turned away and pulled the handkerchief from the breast pocket of his coat. But, with his back to them, he wiped his nose and eyes while saying, "I'd have had you tarred and feathered if you didn't!"

When he turned to face them again, he was smiling, although his vision was still somewhat clouded. "A marvelous day, indeed," he said, bending over to kiss Mia's forehead before disappearing into his study.

Perhaps the happiest person of all, aside from Oliver, Sarah, and Mia, was Layla. She'd been managing the Hutchins household and staff since the untimely passing of Sarah's mother, Olivia, in 1853. At the time, Layla Reese was eighteen years old and had been hired as a maid only one year earlier. When Olivia fell ill, Layla began preparing simple meals for her, which gradually expanded to include quite an amazing selection of recipes for the entire family, taught to Layla by her own mother, Ophelia Reese, the personal chef to Governor George N. Briggs.

Olivia Hutchins was so impressed with Layla's culinary skills that she offered her a permanent position as the family's full-time cook and her own private quarters within the Hutchins estate. Privately, Layla was only five years older than Sarah, and the two of them had become fast friends, and despite the differences in their public social status, they were like sisters.

It was Layla to whom Sarah had first confessed her love for Oliver, and despite Sarah's seemingly never-ending parade of gentleman suitors, Oliver was the only one of whom Layla had ever approved. Their official engagement was like a personal validation for Layla, that her faith in Oliver's loyalty and unwavering commitment to Sarah had been wholly justified.

As happens occasionally when one's focus is concentrated on the positive things surrounding them, there comes a reminder that the evil lurking in the shadows does not go away just because it has been ignored. Oliver and Mia had been in Boston for nearly a half year when they received an urgent dispatch from Sheriff Frederick Walsh in Virginia City, Nevada, informing them that ownership of the property legally transferred to Mia upon the deaths of her parents, Donovan, and Beverly Hampton, was now being contested by surveyors from the Union Pacific Railroad.

According to the dispatch, they were in possession of documents provided by a certain Clifford Kasey, claiming that he had obtained the access rights to the property from her legal guardian, Peter Hampton. Although Sheriff Walsh knew this not to be true and had assured them he'd personally granted legal guardianship of Mia, not to Peter Hampton, but rather to Marshal Oliver Blackstone, both of whom were still duly registered and legal residents of Washoe County in Nevada, the Union Pacific Railroad still refused to back down. After filing a demand letter requesting the court to honor the original land access documents provided by Clifford Kasey prior to his murder, the judge had granted them conditional approval, which would take lawful effect after fourteen days unless formally contested in court by both Mia Hampton and her appointed legal guardian, Marshal Oliver Blackstone.

Ironically, this method of exercising court-sanctioned land grabs had been highly effective prior to 1869, when such short response timeframes would have been impossible to meet. Those very same unscrupulous businessmen who were trying to lay railroad ties across the idyllic piece of land where Mia's house currently stood, had created the very thing that would result in their failure.

They had built the Transcontinental Railroad, and during the next seven days, Mia Hampton and Marshal Oliver Blackstone would use the Union Pacific Railroad's own creation to ensure that they would fail.

At first, when Oliver shared the telegraph dispatch with Sarah, Leonard, and Layla, their hearts collectively sank. However, soon thereafter, they were all filled with the same righteous outrage. How dare they try to take Mia's home, the legacy her father had built for Mia and her mother with his own two hands!

Whether by their direct or indirect involvement, they were attempting to profit from the deaths of Donovan and Beverly Hampton, hoping that anyone legally capable of objecting to their actions would either be unwilling or unable to do so.

For nearly twenty years, Oliver had taken on the monsters that left others trembling in fear. He'd gone after the worst of the worst criminals and outlaws, who believed themselves to be unchallengeable, and he'd challenged and beaten them all.

A little less than forty-eight hours earlier, he and Sarah stood hand in hand, promising Mia that as Donovan and Beverly watched over her from above, they would watch over her here on Earth. This was as much a promise as an oath, and this time when he headed west, he would not be travelling alone, because Mia and Sarah would be with him.

CHAPTER 17

ALTHOUGH IT WAS not the grand wedding that any of them had envisioned, the next afternoon, Oliver and Sarah were married in a private ceremony at the Hutchins estate. That did not mean either Sarah and Mia, or Leonard and Layla, would be denied their lavishly planned and executed social event of the decade. Oliver simply found it improper to drag Sarah to the other end of the continent without them being formally wed.

The preparations for that momentous event would continue unabated, and if anyone believed otherwise, they would have been guilty of drastically underestimating the steely resolve of a devoted Layla Reese. She had been mentally planning Sarah's wedding day for well over a decade, and from her elaborately detailed wedding dress to the veritable bounty of culinary delights, it would be Layla's day to make Sarah shine.

When the three of them boarded the coach at the edge of the estate's sprawling front lawn, both Sarah and Mia looked like royalty. Attired in elegant Victorian dresses, with Leonard and

Oliver holding the French double coach doors open, and Layla following along behind them like a doting step-sister, it was reminiscent of a scene from *Charles Perrault's Cinderella.* When their coach left the compound gates, both Leonard and Layla seemed to view it more as a wedding dress rehearsal than as a simple departure for a short-term, cross-country journey.

Once aboard the train, with their baggage stowed by the porter and swaddled in the luxurious accommodations of the first-class Pullman coach, Sarah's excitement was no less evident than Mia's. The two of them looked more like nervous schoolgirls than Bostonian aristocracy, and Oliver watched in wordless wonder as they embarked upon this exciting adventure together.

Unlike the eastbound journey with Oliver and Mia, the stunning impact of the landscape passing outside the window did not diminish as they traveled westward. Sarah had never ventured farther than Chicago, Illinois, and when they crossed the mighty Mississippi River, the world beyond it was like a magical western wonderland for her. That excitement was also transferred to Mia as the two of them sat riveted to the window, marveling at each new, majestic mountain view.

By the time they left Promontory Point, Utah, on the final leg of their journey, it was questionable in Oliver's mind whether either of them was anxious to return to Boston at all.

When at last they arrived in Reno and stepped out onto the railroad platform, the most notable difference for Sarah was the smell of the surrounding air. It was almost indescribably clean, and after having spent almost a half year in Boston, even Oliver and Mia were keenly aware of the difference.

"The air is crispy here," said Mia, squinting and wrinkling her nose as if trying to understand why there was such a difference.

"That's because here, the dirt is on the ground where it belongs, instead of in the air," said Oliver, stepping up behind Mia and Sarah with his hands on his hips and inhaling deeply.

"What say we head over to the Frontier Hotel to get set up for tonight?" suggested Oliver. "Later, I'll hire us a rig with a couple of horses, and we can set out for Virginia City at first light."

"That sounds wonderful," said Sarah, with an apparent permanent smile etched onto her face.

Despite the dusty streets and sun-bleached pine and spruce buildings lining them, Reno, Nevada had a certain welcoming feel that was intangible yet palpable.

When they entered the doors of the Frontier Hotel, they were barely inside before the barkeep recognized them.

"Well, howdy marshal!" he said, leaning across the bar and extending his hand to Oliver. "It's been some time since your last visit."

"A few months," Oliver replied, shaking the bartender's hand.

"I'd recognize the little lady anywhere," he said, smiling at Mia.

"My name's Mia," she said, "but I don't remember you."

"Well, my name is Paul, but everyone calls me Sam," he said. "The last time you were here, I think you charmed everyone at the hotel. In fact, Annie is going to be thrilled to see you!"

Mia's face lit up at the mention of Annie, and Sam returned his attention to Oliver and Sarah, saying, "And this must be the lovely fiancée you and I were toasting to."

"It is," Oliver replied, smiling as he introduced her, saying, "This is my wife, Sarah Blackstone."

"Well, congratulations, Mr. and Mrs. Blackstone," said Sam, reaching for the bottle of rye whiskey in the decorative glass vitrine behind him.

"It's a little too early for me," said Oliver with a wave. "Perhaps we can revisit that offer after dinner though."

"It'd be an honor," Sam replied, tipping his bowler hat to Sarah, and saying, "And it's a genuine pleasure to meet you, ma'am."

As they turned to walk towards the reception desk, Mia looked curiously at the bartender, asking, "Why do they call you Sam, if your real name is Paul?"

"You know, for the life of me, I can't tell you. Folks have been calling me Sam for nigh on ten years now. I guess everyone remembers Sam, but no one remembers Paul," he answered with a smile.

Apparently satisfied with his explanation, Mia turned and followed Sarah and Oliver, waving back at Sam as they continued across the lobby to the reception desk.

After receiving their keys, they proceeded upstairs to the far end of the third floor, where Mia's room was located directly across the hallway from Oliver and Sarah. While they settled into their rooms to freshen up, Oliver took the opportunity to make extra-special dinner plans before heading over to the livery stable.

The owner recognized the marshal immediately, although for a distinctly different reason than the barkeep. He approached Oliver with a boisterous laugh, saying, "I was hoping you'd be back!"

Eyeing the man suspiciously, Oliver asked, "And just why might that be?"

He didn't even need to wait for a reply, because the ruckus coming from the back of the stables immediately revealed the answer to his question. Upon hearing his voice, the belligerent braying of two ornery mules began to echo through the building and out onto the street in front of it.

"Kate? Buddy?" said Oliver incredulously, walking towards the source of the sounds emanating from the stalls at the rear of the barn. "Well, I'll be damned!" he exclaimed, reaching out to rub each of their faces.

To the owner's astonishment, both animals calmed down immediately, and unlike with anyone else who'd reached into their stalls, neither of the two mules tried to bite him.

"I can't believe you haven't sold them yet," Oliver said, shaking his head in sheer disbelief.

"Oh, I have!" said the amused stable owner. I've sold them a few times, but selling them and keeping them sold are two entirely different matters. I'd sell them, and the next morning, they'd be right back here again, waiting for you. A couple of hours later, an angry customer would be out front yelling at me until I refunded their money!"

Although Oliver was more than happy to buy back his mules, he still couldn't understand why the man was so amused. Reaching into his coat pocket, Oliver said, "How about I just refund your money, along with a fair price for feed and stabling, and we..."

"I couldn't take your money, marshal," said the man, still grinning from ear-to-ear. Oh, I was pissed at first, but after the first couple of times, I started making wagers with Oscar at the hardware store across the street. We'd bet on how long it would take for either the buyers to bring them back or for them to turn up here on their own. Pretty soon, half the town wanted to get in on it, and whether I won or not, we all had one hell of a laugh every time," said the man, slapping his knee and doubling over while wheezing aloud.

Just watching the man's merriment was contagious, and soon, Oliver was laughing right along with him, appearing from a distance as if the two men had been drinking all day. Finally, they collected themselves enough for Oliver to purchase a covered coach.

Walking with Oliver over to a surprisingly well-appointed carriage, the man said, "It's the best one I've got, but it may look a bit strange with two mules pulling it."

"At least the scenery will be familiar," said Oliver, gladly paying the gentleman for the carriage and requesting it be ready to go by 7:00 a.m. the following morning.

By the time he got back to the Frontier Hotel, Sarah and Mia were both ready for dinner, and when they entered the restaurant together, Mia discovered that Sam's prediction had been accurate. Annie's elation was boundless as she and Mia enjoyed a heartwarming reunion at the foot of the stairs. It seemed as if she'd been waiting for that moment since last seeing the endearing child some six months earlier, as she showed the three of them to their seats.

This time, both Sarah and Mia were the pictures of Bostonian etiquette as they dined while wearing their traditional dinner gloves. Thanks to the amazing mentorship of Layla Reese, Mia now knew how to correctly use every piece of dinnerware on the table.

Following their delicious meal of butter-braised venison, baby carrots, and potatoes au gratin, Mia was hoping to share a dessert with Oliver and Sarah. To her delight, that dessert was a miniature chocolate cake. To her surprise, it had eight candles on it.

"Happy birthday, Mia!" exclaimed Sarah and Oliver in unison as Annie placed the delicious looking cake in front of her.

Mia was shocked, and when Sarah said, "Now, you have to make a wish and blow out the candles," instead, she began to cry.

"What's wrong, sweetheart?" asked Oliver, with a consoling smile.

Looking at him, she sobbed, "I don't have anything left to wish for."

Taking her napkin and dabbing Mia's eyes with it, Sarah said, "It's okay, honey." You can save your wish if you want to. "

"Okay," said Mia, nodding and drawing in a deep breath to blow out the candles but stopping just before she exhaled. "Oh, I thought of something," she said, bowing her head and folding her hands together in front of her. A few seconds later, she opened her eyes and blew out every candle in one single breath, to the applause of everyone around their table.

After eating her birthday cake dessert and washing it down with a complimentary glass of cold milk, Mia was understandably exhausted when Sarah and Oliver took her upstairs to her room and tucked her in. She was literally asleep within seconds of her head sinking into the floral-scented pillow. After kissing her goodnight, Sarah and Oliver quietly slipped out of her room and into theirs across the hall.

They had been together for seven years and married for six days. It was only fitting that they spent the next five hours disheveling the bedding of the elaborately-appointed four-poster bed in the Honeymoon Suite of Reno, Nevada's Frontier Hotel.

CHAPTER 18

OLIVER WAS AWAKE by 6:00 a.m., but with Sarah still sleeping peacefully next to him, he was in no hurry to face the chilly temperatures lurking beyond the barrier of the goose-down comforter covering them. Despite that trepidation, he quietly slipped from beneath the sheets and walked over to the window, edging the curtain aside to peer out into the morning grey.

The fog had not yet burned off to reveal what was certain to be a beautiful day, and beyond the pane-glass window, all was peaceful and quiet, far removed from the pre-sunrise buzz of activity beyond the walls of the Hutchins estate in Boston.

Sarah had been secretly admiring the finely-sculpted man at the window for several seconds. "What are you looking at, Mr. Blackstone?" she asked while stretching languorously, as the bedsheet fell away from her.

When he turned from the window to look back, he said, "I honestly don't remember anymore." Walking over to the bed, he cradled her face in his hands and kissed her. When their lips parted, he finished the sentence he'd begun, by adding, "Mrs. Blackstone."

Sarah could only smile, recalling the intensity of their post-nuptial consummation, and longing to revisit those moments often with her ruggedly handsome husband.

"As much as I hate to, we need to get going," said Oliver. With a final kiss to her inviting lips, he said, "Sunrise waits for no one."

Re-focusing his attention on the day ahead, Oliver dressed quickly, with the final articles being his boots, gun belt, and jacket. "I'll be back in half-an-hour to take everything downstairs, then we can have breakfast before we set out for Virginia City," he said, winking at her before closing the door behind him.

The telegraph office opened at 6:00 a.m. sharp, and Oliver was there a few minutes later. After sending a dispatch to notify Sheriff Walsh that they would arrive at approximately 5:00 p.m., and would be staying at the International Hotel, he dropped by the US Marshals Service field office.

"Good morning," he said, knocking on the door as he stepped inside the small building.

Turning abruptly, Deputy Douglas Cherry recognized him right away, saying, "Marshal Blackstone! Welcome back!" Pointing towards one of two chairs at a small round table, he asked, "Coffee?"

"I'll take a cup," Oliver replied, having a seat on one of the two chairs.

As the deputy poured the strong brew into a pewter coffee cup, he asked, "What brings you back to Reno?"

"Oh, I'm here to clear up a property dispute in Virginia City," Marshal Blackstone replied. "It should only take a day or two, so I'll be headed back east to Boston next week."

"But, that's not why you're here," said the deputy, tapping his index finger on the table and raising an eyebrow.

"No. It isn't," said Oliver. After taking a sip of the strong black coffee, he placed the cup on the table and said, "I wanted to see if you have any news regarding the whereabouts of one Charlie Spurlock, also known as the Washoe Kid."

"Not since he murdered Clifford Kasey and shot Sheriff Walsh in Virginia City," said Deputy Cherry. "That kind of attention tends to force people into hiding," he added.

"So does killing ordinary citizens in cold blood, but the last time I was here, he came within an inch of calling me out, and had I not been wearing a marshals badge, he'd have pulled on me without a second thought," said Oliver.

"That sounds like Spurlock," said Deputy Cherry. "He's not much of a talker, and from what I hear, he likes to draw while he's still walking up on you, so if you do see him, don't wait for him to stop and call you out."

"Duly noted," said Oliver.

"Another thing," said the deputy. "According to the sheriff, the man is fast, and I mean deadly fast. The sheriff had a rifle bead on him with his finger on the trigger, and Spurlock still got the drop on him. He's not the kind of gunslinger you want to take on alone," concluded Deputy Cherry.

Oliver stood, and after swirling the final sips around in his mug, he finished his coffee and placed the empty cup on the table, saying, "None of them are." Tipping his hat, he added, "Thank you, deputy," before heading back outside and down the sidewalk towards the Frontier.

Sarah and Mia were already seated in the bistro downstairs when Oliver walked back into the hotel and across the lobby to join them. He'd only been seated for a moment when Annie appeared to fill his coffee cup.

"Breakfast will be out shortly," she said with a smile before dashing off and vanishing into the kitchen.

"So, where did you go this morning?" asked Sarah, not wanting to miss any part of this exciting new experience.

"Well, I went to the telegraph office and sent a dispatch to Sheriff Walsh in Virginia City, letting him know we'll be arriving at around 5:00 p.m., and staying at the International Hotel. After that, I checked in with the US Marshals Service field office to let them know I'll be here in the region for a few days," Oliver explained.

When Oliver mentioned their expected arrival time in Virginia City, Mia immediately began counting on her fingers. Afterwards, she looked curiously at him, and said, "You told me it only takes seven hours to get to Virginia City, but if we leave at seven o'clock and don't get there until five o'clock, then that's ten hours," she said, holding up her fingers as indisputable evidence.

"That's mighty observant of you, Deputy Mia," said Oliver. "But, that doesn't account for the little detour that I have planned," he noted, raising only one eyebrow.

"What kind of detour?" asked Mia, mimicking his expression with her own raised eyebrow.

"Well, I don't want to spoil the surprise, so you'll just have to wait and see," Oliver replied, winking secretively.

As honorary Deputy Mia was about to continue her impromptu interrogation, they were interrupted by a briskly walking Annie, carrying a tray with a huge stack of flapjacks and maple syrup, scrambled eggs, bacon, salt-cured country ham, fried potatoes, freshly baked bread, and a glass of milk for Mia. In her ever-present, delightful manner, she placed the array of dishes and plates onto the large wooden dining table, while saying, "If you need anything else, just holler."

"Who's going to eat all of this?" asked Sarah, in sheer disbelief of the portion sizes. "This could feed a regiment."

"It's a long ride to Virginia City," Annie replied melodically. "What you can't eat now, I'll pack into a basket you can take along for later." Looking suspiciously at Mia, she added, "As long as *you* promise to bring it back."

"I promise," said Mia, smiling as Sarah placed an enormous flapjack onto her plate, and Annie continued on her way back to the kitchen.

As expected, after everyone had eaten their fill, over half of the food was still on the table. Annie seemed to magically appear right on time, carrying a wicker picnic basket, complete with a red and white checkered tablecloth.

Placing the basket onto the empty chair at their table, she quickly folded all of the leftover food into cloth napkins and packed them neatly inside it. She also poured a generous supply of maple syrup into a mason jar, and after sealing it tightly, she squeezed that into the basket as well, finally covering everything with the tablecloth. When she closed and latched the hinged wooden flaps, the contents all fit perfectly.

"See," said Annie. "It was just the right amount."

After thanking her kindly, they all rose from the table with Sarah and Mia hugging Annie before making their way towards the front door. Oliver left two silver dollar coins on the table, collected the bags the bellman had graciously carried down to the lobby for them, and followed Sarah and Mia as they stepped outside.

"Oh my goodness!" exclaimed Sarah upon seeing the luxurious carriage parked in front of the hotel entrance.

Mia was speechless, and just stared at it with an ever-widening grin.

The glossy black carriage was mounted on a leaf-spring suspension with heavy-duty spoked wheels and comfortably cushioned upholstered seats. It featured a convertible top that could be quickly raised and lowered as either shade against a harsh mid-day sun, or shelter in the event of a sudden encounter with inclement weather.

It would have been a stylish ride, even in Boston, were it not for the tandem of oversized pack-animals hitched to it.

Laughing aloud, Sarah asked, "Where on earth did you get those?" while pointing incredulously at the two mules.

"Sarah, meet Kate and Buddy," Oliver said, simulating a bow while gesturing towards the two uncommonly loyal and incredibly intelligent hybrid animals.

"They're huge!" said Sarah, barely able to contain her laughter while asking, "Will we even be able to see anything past those two enormous asses?"

Oliver had to laugh in spite of himself, as he graciously helped both Sarah and Mia into their ornately odd transport combination. A few minutes later, he'd loaded their belongings into the trunk, and after storing his trusty Henry repeater on the mounts affixed to the kickplate beneath the footrest, the trio of travelers were on their merry way.

Due to the relative comfort of the carriage and the breathtaking, panoramic scenery visible despite the two "enormous asses" in front of them, the trip seemed to progress relatively quickly. There were a number of other travelers they encountered along the route, all of whom bore the same perplexed expressions on their faces as the ornate, mule-drawn carriage passed by them.

They were only about five miles from the outskirts of Virginia City, Nevada, and Mia was still dozing when Oliver left the main road, turning onto a narrow, nearly overgrown path. Having never been there before, Sarah had noticed nothing unusual about the slight alteration in their route. Even so, she couldn't help but marvel at the unexpected beauty of their idyllic, storybook surroundings.

Upon cresting a final pine-covered hilltop, an Eden-like paradise unexpectedly zoomed into view. When Oliver stopped the carriage, they were gazing across a secluded meadow running alongside a briskly-flowing, almost crystalline stream. Sarah was leagues beyond stunned when she turned to Oliver with eyes wide in amazement, asking, "Is this *your* place?"

Reaching onto the seat behind them, Oliver gently shook the leg of the sleeping young girl to wake her, before returning his gaze to Sarah.

"No," he said. "It's Mia's."

CHAPTER 19

WHEN MIA SAT up in the back seat of the carriage, she couldn't even comprehend what she was seeing. At first, she thought she was either dreaming now, or had previously concocted the visions of this enchanting place from the pain of missing it so badly. However, it was exactly as she remembered it.

As Oliver drove the carriage down the grass-covered slope, he found himself speechless. The house, the charred remnants of the burnt-out barn and panning stations, and even the rope swing dangling from the uncharacteristic black oak, were all precisely where Mia said they would be.

What was most unexpected was the water. Not only had it returned, but it was nearly a river. During the monsoon season in northern Nevada, it has been known to rain for days on end. Without an unscrupulous Clifford Kasey or his band of unmerry men to repair and maintain the hastily erected dam he'd illegally installed; Mother Nature had reclaimed what was rightfully hers.

Although it had swept away almost all of the barn which had fallen into the nearly dry creek bed during the fire, beforehand, it had utterly destroyed the dam. When the stored kinetic energy of the water trapped inside that manmade reservoir was suddenly released, the ensuing flood swept nearly everything in its path into the snaking ravine beyond it, including Clifford Kasey's house.

Donovan Hampton had wisely observed the levels of the century high watermark before even beginning construction of his home. Much like the bluff overlooking Oliver's Springfield, Massachusetts property, any floodwaters capable of reaching that level would almost certainly require the assistance of Noah in order to escape them.

When Clifford Kasey's dam broke, the raging torrent of surging flood waters had literally purged the ravine of centuries of accumulated debris, effectively widening the natural waterway and allowing the stream to flow much more freely than it had in hundreds of years.

From the hilltop, the house looked like an incredibly large, windowless log cabin with a porch wrapped around it. Were it not for the sturdy wooden steps leading up to what might possibly be deemed an entrance, from that distant location, it would not have been obvious.

As the carriage drew nearer, Mia had been impatiently waiting for Oliver to stop, and even before he could open the carriage door for her, she sprang from it and sprinted directly up the steps. She proceeded down the left wall of the building, stopping after a dozen steps or so and kneeling. Putting her finger into a knotted floor plank, she lifted the board and removed a long, narrow iron rod with a small hook at one end and a ninety-degree curve terminating at a wide metal plate on the other. Then, she replaced the board and ran back to the latchless wall directly in front of the steps and inserted the rod into what appeared to be a bullet hole. Once she had fully inserted the rod, it dropped forward until the metal plate at the other end prevented it from falling inside completely. Next, she turned the metal plate until the rod could be heard clunking against the inner wall. Once gravity had drawn the rod to its final pendular point, she simply pulled it out, unlatching the door from the inside and allowing it to open.

Both Oliver and Sarah were amazed at the speed with which Mia had gained access to the house, and by the unexpectedly intricate latching system securing it. When the door opened, she turned to them excitedly and said, "Come in!"

For a house that had stood empty for nearly six months, it was surprisingly well-kept and remarkably tidy. With the exception of a thin layer of dust coating nearly everything inside, it seemed as if the family living there could be returning at any moment. The heavy wooden exterior blinds, covering the interior windowpanes, were exacting in the precision with which they were fabricated. They covered the vulnerable glass behind them with nary a seam, and could only be unlocked and opened from the inside. Had anyone managed to stumble upon the house while illegally trespassing on the Hampton's property, it would have been easier to burn the entire structure to the ground than it would have been to break into it.

For Oliver, it was clear the barn fire was set after the family had retired for the evening. There were dust-covered plates still positioned neatly on the table, as if pre-set for the next morning's meal, along with coffee cups for Donovan and Beverly, and a milk glass for Mia.

The way the young girl confidently opened the windows and doors to allow sunlight and fresh air into the house was obviously a well-rehearsed routine for her. Once fully illuminated, the painstaking craftsmanship that had gone into creating this magnificent home was nothing short of awe-inspiring.

"Your father did all of this?" asked Oliver, almost unable to believe his own eyes as they wandered from room to room, with Mia leading the way.

"Yes," said Mia. Mom said there weren't many people who were willing to help newcomers like us during the silver war, so Dad did everything himself. I think they liked it better that way, because no one ever bothered us here," Mia explained.

"I can certainly understand that," said Oliver. "My place was barely more than a few pine branches hung over a cave opening. Your dad was truly an amazing builder to have done all of this," Oliver acknowledged, adding, "No wonder he fought so hard to keep it."

Looking down at Mia, he said, "And tomorrow, we're going to make sure that you can keep it too."

They spent nearly two hours at the property, wandering the grounds near the house and up towards the site where the barn had previously stood. Before leaving, they spread out their tablecloth beneath the branches of the non-indigenous black oak, where they enjoyed a late-afternoon meal of delicious leftovers from their breakfast in Reno, and by 4:00 p.m., they had locked up the house and were on their way to Virginia City.

As they crossed over the tree-lined ridge concealing the house from the rest of the world, Mia was still glancing backwards when she asked, "Can we come back again tomorrow?"

Taking Oliver's hand and squeezing it, Sarah answered Mia's question by asking one of her own. "Starting tomorrow, Mia, would you mind if we stayed with you for the rest of our trip?"

Mia nearly climbed into the front seat of the carriage with them, hugging both their necks from behind and saying, "You can stay for as long as you want; even forever if you'd like!"

It took less than an hour for them to reach Virginia City, and shortly before 5:00 p.m., they were pulling up to the front of the International Hotel. After offloading their luggage onto the bellman's cart, the young man wheeled it into the lobby, where an astonished hospitality agent named Alfred nearly passed out upon seeing them.

Once he'd regained his composure, he extended his hand, saying, "Welcome back, Marshal."

"Blackstone. Oliver Blackstone, and this is my wife Sarah, and our daughter Mia," said Oliver, cordially.

Nodding politely, the man said, "Well, my name is Alfred, and it's such a pleasure to meet you, Mrs. Blackstone, and so nice to see you again, Mia."

With barely a pause, he slid a key across the countertop to Oliver, saying, "This is for our family suite at the far end of the third floor." I trust you'll be comfortable there, but if you should need anything else, and I do mean anything, just say the word. "

"Thank you, Alfred," said Oliver, reaching into his jacket, removing his US Marshals Service courier purse, and handing it to him. "Would you mind storing this in your vault for me this evening?" he asked.

"I'd be happy to," said Alfred, accepting the pouch and carrying it into the office behind the reception counter.

Immediately thereafter, Oliver, Sarah, and Mia followed the bellman to their suite. When he opened the door and ushered them inside, despite the lavish accoutrements, spacious floorplan, and separate sleeping chambers, they were literally all too tired to even notice.

Oliver departed only briefly to drop off the mules and carriage at the livery stable across the street, and when he returned to the room, both Mia and Sarah were in bed, sleeping soundly. Minutes later, so was Oliver.

The next morning, they awoke exceptionally early after having slept for over ten uninterrupted hours. The long carriage ride, the enchanting detour, and the fresh mountain air coming in from across the Sierra Nevadas had all combined to exhaust the three of them. However, now that they were all well-rested, the exciting day ahead couldn't commence soon enough.

Sarah's first order of business was to make a list of cleaning items needed to get the house into its former pristine condition, along with some rations and supplies to tide them over for the next few days. Beverly's meticulous daily care had been missing for six months, and a deep cleaning would be necessary to remove the dust and restore the luster of the various wooden and glass surfaces. There were also undoubtedly a number of personal items that would have belonged to Donovan and Beverly, and Sarah also wished to purchase a large chest in which those items could be safely stored specifically for Mia to revisit once she was old enough to understand them.

By the time the list was finished, and their plan of attack was set, breakfast was being served in the hotel restaurant. Despite the big day ahead of them, none of them really had much of an appetite, and following a meager breakfast of hot buttered biscuits with strawberry preserves, coffee for Sarah and Oliver, and cold milk for Mia, Oliver collected the carriage and mules for a short drive down to Main Street, the primary thoroughfare for those entering or leaving town at its northwestern-most access point. It was also where the sheriff's office was located, and within walking distance of the courthouse, where Marshal Oliver Blackstone and Miss Mia Hampton would need to appear in order to contest the demand letter submitted by the Union Pacific Railroad.

It was shortly after 8:00 a.m., when Oliver knocked on the jailhouse door and stepped into Sheriff Walsh's office with Mia and Sarah, saying, "Good morning, Sheriff Walsh!"

"Marshal Blackstone!" exclaimed the sheriff, rising to his feet to greet Oliver with a heartfelt handshake. Afterwards, he looked at Mia with a scrutinizing gaze, saying, "There's no way that this charming young lady can be Mia Hampton. She couldn't possibly have grown that much in such a brief time. "

"But, it is me!" exclaimed Mia. "I'm just bigger because now I'm eight," she added.

"Well, I'll take you at your word for that, and I'm sure the judge will too!" said the sheriff, placing his hand reassuringly on her shoulder before turning to face Oliver and Sarah.

"And this must be the new Mrs. Blackstone," said the sheriff cordially.

"She is indeed," said Oliver with a smile, adding, "Sheriff Walsh, meet Sarah Blackstone." Sarah, this is the legendary sheriff of Virginia City, Sheriff Frederick Walsh. "

"It's a genuine pleasure to meet you, sheriff," said Sarah, extending her hand to him.

Accepting and shaking it gently, Sheriff Walsh said, "Mrs. Blackstone, that pleasure is, without question, entirely mine."

The sheriff turned back towards Oliver and said, "I was glad to hear you got that bloodthirsty psychopath who was stalking you back in Boston." I hear he was suspected of close to fifty murders, and I honestly believe he may have been part of the failed Lincoln assassination attempt back in 1861. "

"After personally witnessing how he could weasel his way in close to his victims, I would not have put anything past him. I guess I'm fortunate to have gotten away with only a very close shave!" said Oliver.

Looking down at his pocket watch, the sheriff said, "Speaking of cutting it close, we're nowhere near that, but how about we head over to the courthouse so we can piss all over... I mean, put an end to Union Pacific's shameful behavior?"

"Just lead the way," said Oliver, taking one of Mia's hands while Sarah held the other.

Although it seemed to be an overly cautious measure, just outside the door, there were now four of the sheriff's deputies waiting to escort Oliver, Mia, and Sarah to the courthouse, with the sheriff himself walking ahead out in front of them. It was meant to be a statement by Sheriff Walsh, and it was absolutely delivered and taken as such without ambiguity by the railroad's lawyers when the protective detail marched right past them, up the stairs, and into the courthouse.

The railroad's catalogue of intimidation and distraction tactics all evaporated when Oliver and Mia showed up, twenty minutes ahead of their appointment time. Furthermore, their planned strategic objection to Marshal Blackstone serving as Mia's legal guardian due to a lack of a female presence in the household crumbled like a sandcastle when both of Mia's newly adoptive parents were suddenly present for the hearing.

When the bailiff called them into the courtroom to present their statements, the judge simply asked, "In the matter of the Union Pacific Railroad versus Mia Louise Hampton and her legal guardian, Marshal Oliver James Blackstone, duly appointed as such by the elected sheriff of Washoe County, Nevada, Mr. Frederick Arnold Walsh, and with the signed approval of this very magistrate, regarding the unrestricted access rights to the land bequeathed unto Mia Hampton in the sealed and certified last will and testaments of both Donovan Lee Hampton and Beverly Mae Hampton, what say you both?"

Nodding in sync, as if counting down from three, both Mia and Oliver boldly declared simultaneously, "I object!"

Five minutes later, the surveyors for the Union Pacific Railroad in Provo, Utah, received an urgent dispatch from their attorney in Virginia City, Nevada, which read: "Plans for northern survey zone-1 are hereby terminated (stop). Implement immediate advancement of southern survey zone-2 (Full Stop). "

CHAPTER 20

THOSE WHO HAD witnessed the overwhelming show of force put on display by Sheriff Walsh and his exceptionally capable deputies were notably impressed. During their victory procession back to the sheriff's office, a man named Jesse Bartlett had been waiting just beyond the foot of the courthouse steps. He was, by chance, that same prospector who voluntarily accessorized the right boot of Clifford Kasey following his arrest.

When the railroad's attorneys left the courthouse in a huff, and the sheriff's entourage emerged, the looks on the faces of Oliver, Sarah, and Mia told the story that spoken words never could have.

"They won!" screamed the elated Jesse Bartlett, rushing down the dusty street on his skinny bowlegs. "Goddammit! They done beat the railroad!"

As the unofficial town crier rushed ahead to announce the judge's decision, dozens of merchants, and residents along both sides of the street stepped out onto the sidewalks and balconies to applaud them as they passed. The celebratory feeling in the air was extraordinary; however, it wasn't shared by everyone.

Although he may have been the sole exception, Charlie Spurlock was unimpressed by the triumph being celebrated among everyone else around him. He'd been waiting inside an alleyway that opened up into the bordering prairie northeast of Main Street. From there, he would have had a clear escape route into the foothills of the Sierra Nevada Mountain Range after gunning down Sheriff Walsh, Mia Hampton, and Marshal Blackstone.

The veritable army of rifle-wielding, highly alert deputies had quickly altered his lofty and presumptuous plan. He had arrogantly believed this to be the best opportunity he would ever have to take them all down at once. Rather fortunately or unfortunately, depending on an individual's unique perspective, that plan had been successfully foiled by the sheriff's well-prepared brigade of law enforcement professionals.

Back inside the sheriff's office, Oliver said, "Thank you, Sheriff Walsh, for everything."

"Awww, don't mention it," Sheriff Walsh replied, shaking Oliver's hand, and then laying a congratulatory one on Mia's shoulder and saying, "Sometimes, the good guys actually win."

"You and your men are quite an impressive team," Sarah noted, adding, "I must admit, I've never felt more secure."

"Well, once a Pinkerton, always a Pinkerton," replied the sheriff. "In my view, prevention will always trump confrontation, and I was recently reminded that not everyone deserves a fair fight."

"True words of wisdom," said Oliver, nodding in agreement.

"Would you like my boys to escort you back to the international?" "It wouldn't be a problem," suggested Sheriff Walsh.

"That won't be necessary," said Oliver. "With the amount of attention focused on the three of us, Virginia City may just be the safest place on Earth right now."

"I'm sure you're right," replied the sheriff, adding, "I hope you enjoy your stay, and if any of you ever need anything, you can always count on me."

"Of that, I have no doubt," said Oliver, urging on Buddy and Kate and resuming their impromptu parade back in the direction of the International Hotel.

The Washoe Kid had vacated the city shortly after the streets had begun to fill with the curious onlookers lured outside by the boisterous announcement, trumpeted victoriously by Jesse Bartlett. Accordingly, Oliver's and the sheriff's predictions had been correct. The sheer number of people gathering along the sidewalks, hoping to get a look at the little girl who had just beaten back the Union Pacific, made it impossible to target them with anything but adoration.

It was only 10:00 a.m. when they pulled up outside the storefront of J&K Gunsmiths of Virginia City. At first, Auntie Karen was somewhat taken aback by the unusual chariot, pulled into view by two abnormally large mules. However, when Oliver stepped down to open the carriage door for Sarah and Mia, Karen rushed out the front entrance to meet them, even before they'd reached the ground.

"Oliver!" she shouted merrily, as he advanced up the porch steps to greet her.

"Auntie Karen!" responded Oliver, hugging her tightly. Following their embrace, he walked back to help Sarah and Mia up the wooden steps, saying, "This is my aunt, Karen Martel, and Auntie Karen." These two are my wife, Sarah, and our daughter, Mia. "

"Well, be still my beating heart," Karen gasped aloud, first taking Sarah into her arms and saying, "You are the literal image of grace and beauty," before looking at Oliver to claim, "I've always said you would marry the fairest maiden in the land."

As both Sarah and Oliver stood together arm-in-arm quietly observing, Karen slowly turned to look at Mia. Moving cautiously towards the politely patient child, as if to prevent any sudden wind shift that might inadvertently dispel the mirage-like vision in front of her, she said, in barely more than a whisper, "I swear to God, I have just beheld my first angel."

As Karen leaned over Mia with her hands clasped together in front of her, indicative of her delightful nature, Mia extended her hand, saying, "It's very nice to meet you, Auntie Karen."

Bypassing the cordial handshake, Karen used Mia's extended arm to draw the charming young lady into her loving embrace, saying, "And I have wished for so long to meet you!"

Standing and wiping tears of joy from her eyes and cheeks, triggered by the unexpected yet wonderful surprise, Karen said, "Please come inside and sit with me for a spell."

Once inside the store, she flipped the sign on the door, indicating they were closed, then ushered the trio through the veritable museum of firearms history. The aromas of leather, gun oil, blued steel, carved wooden rifle stocks and pistol grips, brass, lead, and gunpowder, all combined to create the unique atmosphere that those who had never ventured west of the Mississippi would find nearly impossible to comprehend.

In Sarah's former fanciful imaginings, that smell was the western frontier she'd envisioned while being enraptured by the tales of returning pioneers and daring frontiersmen. The dramatic high-noon showdowns, wilderness confrontations with dangerous animals, and a seemingly never-ending array of firearms with which the West was allegedly won, were all gathered here in stunning reality.

Although Mia had spent most of her life near Virginia City, this kind of establishment was an unexplored adventure for her. Aside from her dad's single-shot Spencer carbine for hunting large game, an ancient double-barreled shotgun for squirrels and rabbits, and a Remington.44 Army Revolver, Mia had been nearly unacquainted with guns prior to those fateful events preceding her introduction to Oliver. In fact, she'd only rarely even heard gunfire.

Donovan would kill, dress, salt, and smoke one elk, a deer or two, a wild boar, and a single bighorn sheep each year. Those, along with small game and waterfowl, were never hunted near the house, and other than a rattlesnake Beverly once discovered near the porch steps, Mia had never seen him kill anything. Donovan simply believed that if he wasn't going to eat it, he didn't need to kill it.

After the protracted tour of Karen's gun shop, they finally made their way into the living quarters at the rear of the building, where the tempting aroma of her delicious caramel rolls clung to the air in sharp contrast to those out front in the store. While partaking of the delectable baked bread, still warm from the oven, Karen regaled Sarah and Mia with stories of Oliver's rambunctious boyhood.

Her eldest sister, Abigail, was James Blackstone's second wife, and he was nearly sixty years old when they married. They'd lived in Texas since the 1820s, when Oliver's father served as an ambassador between the fracturing Mexican government and the Anglo Texan immigrants moving there in ever-increasing numbers.

After attempting to conceive for a number of years, Abigail eventually became pregnant, quite unexpectedly, at the age of thirty-eight. They were looking forward to welcoming their first child when Abigail contracted winter fever, eight months into the pregnancy. She managed to hang on for nearly a month after Oliver was born, but the pneumonia proved too difficult for her to fight off in her weakened condition, and she died in her sleep with Oliver at her breast.

"No one believed he was going to make it," said Karen. But he was a fighter. He always has been. Just like you, Mia. "

Mia smiled as she absorbed the history of a man she'd only known for six months yet loved from nearly the moment she'd met him.

"When Oliver came to us, James's health had already started to fail, and rather than leaving him in the hands of a nanny, I told Jedediah that we were taking him, and that's that!"

Shaking her head in recollection, Karen said, "Oh, he fussed about it at first, but when Oliver started following him around and trying to copy everything he did, Old Jedd Martel's heart turned soft as a cotton ball. By the time Oliver was ten, he could take apart and reassemble every gun out there in that store, and could shoot most of them better than his uncle," Karen raved on.

"I hate to interrupt the unauthorized biography of Oliver Blackstone," said Oliver, smiling. "But, Auntie Karen could go on for hours without taking a break, and we've got a lot to do before we lose the sunlight," he added.

"Awww," said Mia, "I like Auntie Karen's stories!"

"Well, precious, you can come back whenever you want, and I'll tell you everything about little Ollie Blackstone," Karen promised.

Mia beamed up at him with her eyes wide and her mouth agape. "Ollie?" They called you Ollie?"

"Not since I was your age," said Oliver, reminding her, "and on that note, I think we'd best be on our way."

It was nearly noon when they bid Karen a fond farewell, promising to return for more stories. Upon stopping by the International Hotel across the street to check out and pick up their belongings, Oliver settled their bill and collected his leather courier purse from Alfred, before departing with Sarah and Mia.

"What do you keep in there?" asked Sarah, having wondered about it a number of times since their arrival.

"Sometimes a lot, and at other times, like today, nearly nothing," said Oliver. Looking at Sarah, he explained, "At hotels frequented by marshals, we'll leave a pouch like this with the reception, not because the contents of it are confidential, but rather because the marshal who handed it to them wishes for his presence there to remain confidential."

"How do you know they won't tell anyone?" curiously asked Sarah.

"Because we don't use it at every hotel, and we don't use it with every receptionist," stated Oliver. I have known Alfred for over a dozen years, and the last time I was here, he didn't even recognize me when I came through the door with Mia. "The moment he accepted that pouch, none of that mattered, because he had a sacred obligation to honor the request, whether he recognized me or not," Oliver explained.

"And you could trust him just like that?" queried Sarah.

That night, there were at least a half-dozen gunslingers and hired killers looking for us all over Virginia City. "They checked every saloon and every hotel, and at least two of them went in and out of the International while I watched from Auntie Karen's loft across the street," Oliver explained before concluding, "He honored the code, even when he could have chosen not to." He's a good man, and yes. I trust him. "

"Amazing," said Sarah. "We just got off of the train two days ago, and I've already learned more about the western frontier since that time than I ever thought possible."

As they approached Main Street, headed for the General Store, Sarah's curiosity got the better of her again, and she asked Oliver, "What would you have done had he not kept your secret?"

Looking towards Mia on the back seat, Oliver winked and said, "I would have told him my name."

CHAPTER 21

LARS AND EVA Madsen's general store had everything Oliver and Sarah needed to get Mia's family home into shape. Everything, that is, except for the nearly two hours of time they expended completing a twenty-dollar order of ordinary cleaning products and assorted dry goods.

Even though Sarah's list was relatively straightforward, Eva Madsen's detailed usage instructions for nearly every item purchased were unnecessary. From standard lye soap and pine oil to lime for the privy and wood stain for the porch, Eva felt compelled to explain each product in almost granular detail, convinced that such an inexperienced city girl from Boston would be completely lost without her entry-level training lectures.

Finally, Lars politely interrupted her extended sanitation seminar, stating, "Eva, I believe these nice people will be able to figure out how to use a broom, a mop, an assortment of towels and brushes, some soap, a few buckets, and sacks of beans, coffee, and flour, but only if they make it home with enough remaining daylight to do so."

Eva's expression immediately soured; however, Lars's statement had curtailed the fifth recitation of her well-rehearsed soliloquy, and within minutes, the Blackstone family was underway with plenty of sunlight remaining to reach the house and to organize everything for a fresh start the next morning.

Due to their somewhat later than planned arrival, it was almost as if they were picking up where they had left off the previous day. Even knowing what to expect had no significant effect on the impact of the breathtaking view awaiting them from the tree-lined overlook, and that same feeling of incredulity returned with renewed intensity.

It really was perfect, and now, it was also safe from the threat of being buried beneath railroad trestles.

After unloading the supplies from the ornate carriage, Oliver parked it on the far side of the house before unhitching the mules and allowing them to graze freely. Since mules are somewhat territorial, they learn to adapt to the other animals in their environment and quickly become protective of them. Due to their emotional attachment to Oliver, the likelihood of them wandering off was also negligible, and on top of everything else, they were excellent sentinels.

The water well that Mia told them about was located halfway between the house and the site of the former barn, and the water inside it was clear, ice cold, and perfect for boiling potatoes, carrots, wild green onions, and salt pork for a quick and simple dinner stew.

After drawing the water and pouring it into a large cast-iron kettle, he secured the water bucket and set the kettle on the edge of the well for a moment, then walked over to the swiftly flowing creek. Although all of the wooden elements had been washed away during the flood, the remnants of multiple stone foundations were still visible at various points along the banks on both sides of the stream. Noting this, Oliver carried the kettle of water back into the house and attached it to the hook over the fire he'd built in the fireplace.

Sarah and Mia were chopping the vegetables together at a small table in the kitchen when Oliver entered. The scene was surprisingly beautiful in its simplicity, causing him to pause for a moment just to appreciate it.

Smiling to himself, he returned to the question still swirling in his mind and asked, "Mia, honey, do you know what the flat stones out near the edge of the creek are for?"

Furrowing her brow as if straining to remember, Mia replied, "One was for the wash house where mom cleaned our clothes, and there was another one where we could take a bath in warm water." I think Dad was building something new too. He made lots of things because he was an Indian ear," Mia replied. "I'm not sure what it was going to be, but there's a big brown book with pictures, and he would draw them inside it whenever he made something new," she added.

"Can you show me, sweetheart?" Oliver asked, highly intrigued.

Without a word, she dashed into the living room and over to the secretary's desk hutch in the far corner. Oliver followed and watched as she removed a key from the top right-hand drawer, unlocked, and lowered the desktop, then reached inside to retrieve the book of which she'd spoken. After turning and handing it to Oliver, she went back into the kitchen to continue helping Sarah.

The upholstered wooden chair next to the hutch indicated that this had been Donovan's creative workspace, and positioning it in front of the desk, Oliver sat down and opened the cover of the oversized leatherbound ledger. Although he realized Mia had meant to say "engineer" instead of "Indian ear," he was in no way prepared for the information documented inside Donovan's schematic journal.

From the unique locking system for the front door to the barn where his horses and the dairy cow were stabled, Donovan had documented everything to a degree of detail that would have made Eva Madsen blush. Most astounding was the way he carefully illustrated the methods used for building such complex structures, and that nearly all of the work could be performed by a single individual using an array of leverage techniques and, at most, a single horse.

As Mia had recalled, the smaller of the four stone slabs were for a laundry shed and a heated bath house, both of which were approximately the same size. Although the washtubs for the laundry shed and the cast-iron stove and wooden tub inside the bathhouse had all been swept from their foundations, the methods for reconstructing them were all right in front of Oliver, illustrated in amazing detail.

He had purchased the stone slabs from one of the mining companies working the Comstock Lode, and trailered them in, one at a time. Each slab must have weighed at least a ton, yet his ledger explained how he'd positioned them using little more than a rope, a horse, and a half-dozen rounded fence-posts.

For obvious reasons, there was even a self-constructed septic system buried downhill from the privy, preventing it from ever needing to be relocated. The sloped area directly beneath the seat carried the waste directly downhill and away from the outhouse, directly into the septic tank. By keeping a bucket of water handy from either the well or the stream, the underground trough could be rinsed clean after each use, and with the occasional application of lime, nearly all of the accompanying odor could be eliminated.

Oliver realized that the house and the entire property upon which it stood was quite literally a proving ground for the inventions of Donovan Hampton, and despite its isolated location, it was anything but primitive. By the time Mia came over to tell him that dinner was ready, the sun had set, and Oliver had completely lost track of the time and everything else around him, but his mind was almost humming.

"Mia, your father was probably one of the most brilliant men in the country," Oliver stated in respectful acknowledgment. "This house, and so many things about it, are so unique that your dad actually had them registered with the United States Patent and Trademark Office," he added while reading directly from the text inside the ledger.

Looking up at a smiling Sarah, standing directly behind Mia, Oliver said, "Had the railroad company taken over this land, everything here would have been lost."

"Well, obviously, it's why you're here. So that... wouldn't happen." Sarah replied.

As the three of them sat down for an unexpectedly delicious dinner, they were all tired, but also anxious to get started working on the house the next day. Once they had eaten and cleaned up the kitchen and dining room, they moved out onto the elevated porch to enjoy the moonlit serenity surrounding them.

While they were discussing which of their projects to tackle first, three shadowy figures emerged from the tree-lined overlook and slowly moved across the grassy slope opposite the house. Sarah first noticed Oliver's and then Mia's gazes in that direction, and when she turned and saw them for herself, she was on the verge of panicking when Oliver reached over and gently placed his hand on hers.

Midway across the hillside, one very large and two substantially smaller wolves stopped in the gently swaying grass across from where they sat, apparently staring directly at them. After several seconds of motionless silence, the apex predators resumed their trek across the moonlit meadow, before once again disappearing into the surrounding trees.

Finally breaking the almost hypnotic effect of a forest that had suddenly gone completely quiet, Mia whispered, "The puppies are bigger now."

It had been over six months since Oliver had seen them, but he recognized them right away. The mama wolf and her tiny cubs, who had once shared the safety of their den with a frightened little girl, had obviously not forgotten either and did not pose a threat to any of them. Even Buddy and Kate had been un alarmed by their presence, sensing not even the slightest hint of danger directed towards them.

"Have they always been here?" Sarah wondered aloud, still shaken by her first encounter with the villain of so many childhood fairytales from the eighteenth and nineteenth centuries.

"Dad found the mama caught in a snare that someone else put on our property," said Mia. "She almost died because she couldn't get loose or make it to the water, so he cut the wire and carried her over to the creek where she could drink, and when he came back later, she was gone."

Pointing upstream, Mia said, "Sometimes, she would come to the barn up there, and dad would give her food because she was too skinny, but once her paw was better, we would only see her over there on the hill, and she never came over to the house, or the barn after that."

Sarah looked as if Mia were reciting a horror story. There were few things she feared more than wolves after hearing fables of *The Three Little Pigs* and *Red Riding Hood* as a child, not to mention contemporary European folklore regarding werewolves, which she had read as an adult.

"Your father was a very brave man," said Sarah. "I can't imagine coming even one inch closer than we did tonight to such a dangerous creature."

"Dad always said that there was plenty of room for everyone and everything living out here, and as long as we don't bother them, they won't bother us," concluded Mia, before quickly amending her statement and saying, "Except for the rattlesnakes." You can never trust a rattlesnake!"

"I suppose you're right," said Sarah. "As beautiful as this place is, it's still all very new to me. I guess I'll just have to learn to appreciate things for what they are, and not give into my fears of what they might be," she added, taking Oliver's arm, and leaning her head against his shoulder.

Although Oliver had been conspicuously silent during their discussion, he had been anything but distracted. Experience had taught him to pay close attention to those little pearls of wisdom Mia innocently dropped into conversations when recalling details of the memories emblazoned in her mind. He'd also learned to associate potentially ominous events with the subtle warnings that had foreshadowed them.

While Mia and her family clearly had an established history with that female wolf and her growing cubs, Oliver had only seen her on two previous occasions, and following each of them, Mia had been in grave danger, and blood had been shed. Tonight, that wolf had once again stared into Oliver's eyes, and despite their idyllic surroundings, there were clouds on the horizon, and the storm was coming.

CHAPTER 22

THEY WERE THREE days into the cleaning process when Sarah suddenly stopped. An odd sense of uncertainty shot through her as she stood near the bedroom window on the north end of the house, peering out towards the road leading in from the tree line.

Mia was screaming at the top of her lungs, running down the grassy slope as fast as she could when Oliver appeared on the hilltop twenty yards behind her. She was nearly at the wagon path when suddenly, Oliver caught up to her from behind, lifting her into the air and twirling around with her until they both fell to the ground, laughing, dizzy, and out of breath.

After watching them lie there in the tall grass for several minutes, staring up into a perfect Indian summer sky, she walked out onto the porch and yelled, "Oliver and Mia Blackstone! Get over here right now!"

Both of them immediately sprang to their feet, and sprinted the remaining distance from the hillside to the house.

"Yes, ma'am!" said Mia, arriving first.

"Yes, ma'am!" repeated Oliver, arriving close behind her.

"I need you both to see this!" she said, excitedly rushing into the house with Mia and Oliver directly on her heels. When they came through the door, she was in the living room, spinning in her own dizzying little circle with outstretched arms, singing melodically, "We're all done!"

Sarah's unconstrained celebratory outburst had left her at risk of falling herself, so she stopped and took both their hands. She led them from room to room as they dragged their critical fingertips over surfaces previously covered with stubborn dust and grime. She rested her case, proclaiming that the house, from ceiling to floor, and wall to wall, was spotless! With all of the cleaning supplies now stored in their proper places and no longer contributing to the clutter inside, the house was now spacious and welcoming.

There were three sprawling bedrooms, all of equal dimensions, and each of them was equally well furnished. Mia's bedroom was located next door to Donovan's and Beverly's at the southern end of the house, and the guestroom at the northern end was where Oliver and Sarah now slept. Despite the dust that had covered nearly everything else in the house, the linens, and bedcovers in the moth ball-treated cedar chests at the foot of each bed seemed as fresh as they had been the day they were taken from the clothesline.

Out of their abundant respect for Mia and her late parents, all of the personal effects, diaries, important historical documents, valuables, and keepsakes from their bedroom had been collected and carefully stored inside the large cedar trunk they'd purchased specifically for that purpose. After locking it, the trunk was stored in Mia's bedroom, and she was given the only two keys that would open it.

The house was far too beautiful for any part of it to be treated as a mausoleum, and now, it would become an enduring tribute to the amazing man and woman who'd created this lasting legacy for their daughter.

Each day, as they progressed from room-to-room, more of Donovan's ingenuity had been incrementally revealed, and each of his newly-engineered inventions had already been registered for patent protection. Had he never panned for another ounce of ore, the royalties from his inventions alone (to say nothing of their derivative technologies) would have provided a never-ending revenue stream, likely enduring beyond the lifespans of Mia's great-grandchildren's great grandchildren.

Of course, Donovan didn't stop panning for gold. At least, not until Clifford Kasey's dam had interrupted the water flow. Before that, he'd accumulated enough gold to purchase over one hundred acres of land surrounding their private refuge, finance all of his engineering inventions, settle all of his and Beverly's debts in Boston, and become completely independent of a father and brother who had severed ties and disowned him for his apparent lunacy. Beyond that, he'd stored close to a million dollars' worth of gold and silver in a vault beneath the house, which was, again, protected by a proprietary key that, aside from Donovan and Beverly, only Mia knew where to find and how to use.

Upon closer inspection of the foundation stones near the creek, Oliver made another amazing discovery that Donovan and Beverly had unfortunately not lived long enough to see. Following the dam break and ensuing flood during the torrential rains of the monsoon season, a thousand years of earth, rock, and debris were suddenly flushed from the ravine over a period of several days, leaving the lower flood plain covered for nearly eight weeks before it finally receded.

Although much of Donovan's work had been destroyed by the flood, including the elaborate hydro-mechanical panning system he'd devised, which made collecting gold ore nearly as simple as gathering eggs from the henhouse each morning, the benefits in the wake of the cataclysm had been far greater.

There was now so much gold in the shallows along the creek bed that it could easily be seen in the water with the naked eye. It was literally everywhere!

A few miles beyond Mia's property, the walls of the ravine became steeper, forcing the stream into an ever-narrowing creek and eventually into a brook that vanished into a nondescript cavern. While the water inside the cavern was now barely more than a trickle, for nearly two months it had been a veritable subterranean river, laden with gold at its termination point, where the water seeped into the ground and merged with the underlying aquifer. The gold carried into that cave was so abundant that it could have easily been gathered by hand!

Although the parcel at that end of the now barren ravine belonged to a different owner, there was absolutely nothing special about it. In fact, it was little more than a few pine branches hung over a cave opening.

With only two nights remaining before their temporary return trip to Boston, the storm clouds that had been rolling in across the Sierra Nevada Mountains brought with them an unnatural chill in the air.

It was shortly before dusk, and Sarah and Mia were inside reading from Beverly's collection of early American literature. Oliver was up near the tree line, gathering firewood in anticipation of the chilly night ahead of them.

The distinct howl of the mother wolf preceded the sound of the approaching horse hooves by only a few seconds as a rider approached from the northeast and slowed his graceful black mare to a trot, and then to a near-silent walk. Twenty feet before reaching the overlook summit, Charlie Spurlock brought the horse to a complete stop but remained astride it.

From there, he could see the house below without revealing his silhouette within the trees. He was careful. He was very careful.

The two mules grazing in the pasture across from the house would no doubt begin to bray the very moment they realized he was there, so he was quiet. He was very quiet.

He could hear the woman and the young girl laughing inside the house, as there was little other than the sound of the rushing stream to cover their voices as they echoed softly from the surrounding hillsides. Their voices were so peaceful. They were so peaceful and unsuspecting.

He had watched this house from almost exactly the same location over six months ago. The last time, Kasey's men waited until dark before setting the barn ablaze, hoping to strike fear into their hearts and make them leave. But Spurlock knew they weren't afraid that night, and they wouldn't be afraid the next morning, or the morning after that. People like the

Hamptons were tired of running, and they were either standing their ground or they would die on it.

After Blink Masterson and his outlaw renegades had ridden past him over this hill, Spurlock had remained behind, because he knew they would head straight to the sheriff in Virginia City, and Kasey hadn't hired him to burn down their barn; that was Blink Masterson's job. Spurlock was hired to kill them, and that's what he had done.

The only thing Masterson had to do was take care of the kid. A braggadocios gunslinger and five hired guns, and they couldn't even find a barefoot little girl wandering through the woods in the dark. Now, they were all dead, and tonight, he was going to clean up the mess he should never have trusted a lesser man to handle in the first place.

Leaving her alive was now a mistake that had been riding him like walking pneumonia, and tonight, he was putting an end to it.

With a final glance down into the valley, Spurlock took a deep breath and dismounted the mare. The instant his foot touched the ground, a revolver flashed thirty feet away, and a bullet slammed into his thigh, just below the bottom edge of his holster.

"Son of a bitch!" screamed Spurlock as he dropped to the ground next to his still-calm mare. When he looked to his right, Marshal

Blackstone was just standing there, with the tails of his long oilskin coat pulled around behind his body and draped almost casually over his left forearm, exposing the holstered colt on his right hip.

"I've heard that you like to draw on people while you're still walking up to them," said the marshal. "Since I've taken that option away from you, there's no need for this to go any further."

Gritting his teeth and pulling himself back up to his feet while holding onto his horse, Spurlock said, "Well, I've heard that you were a damned coward who didn't give Blink Masterson a fair chance." Now, I believe that was true. "

"You're wanted dead or alive, Spurlock," said Oliver. "I could have put a bullet in your head while you were enjoying the scenery and called it a night, but I didn't."

"And why didn't you?" spat Spurlock, venomously. "Are you chicken shit or just plain yellow?"

"Men like you don't scare me," said Oliver, almost too calmly. "The reason you're still alive is because I want to kill you so badly that I can taste it. Ever since I saw you riding off in Reno six months ago, I've wanted to put a bullet right between your goddamned eyes. I've dreamt about it every night since then, hoping... no... praying, that you would cross my path just one more time; just one more goddamned time! Even at this very instant, I want to kill you so badly that I can feel it in my bones; and just the mention of your accursed name already chambers a round in my mind, and that round always has your shitty face on it. "

Spurlock knew that the marshal was right about his dueling preference. He was faster when he could draw on the move, with his right leg travelling back as his arm was swinging forward past his holster. But that's not what won him the title "The Washoe Kid." He'd earned that name by dropping more than a dozen men while standing across from them, looking them dead in the eyes.

"Well, marshal," Spurlock hissed, stepping away from his horse and lining himself up with Oliver. Locking gazes, his expression went blank, and he said, "Maybe you need to let that bullet find its mark. You know... get it out of your system." An instant later, his hand dropped towards the pearl-handled Colt strapped to his thigh.

Dammit, he was fast! The barrel of the customized Peacemaker cleared the flashy studded holster with a speed that defied all logic, and immediately fell to the ground as his right shoulder socket shattered, and he tumbled backwards onto the pine-needle-covered forest floor.

While still in mid-fall, Charlie Spurlock could see Marshal Blackstone through the gun smoke lingering in the air, standing directly across from him with his Colt already re-holstered and the tails of his oilskin overcoat still draped casually over his left arm.

"We could do this all night, Spurlock," said Oliver. "You could keep getting back up, and I could keep knocking you right back down again."

"So what are you waiting for, you son of a bitch?" screamed Spurlock as he lay there writhing in pain. "Goddamn you, finish it!"

"During the past six months, I've only fired nine bullets and sent seven men just like you to meet their makers, and not one of them did I actually want to kill," said Oliver.

"On the other hand, I want to kill you. Not because you're guilty, even though you are, but because I actually hate you. I despise the wretched womb that allowed a murderous piece of filth like you to crawl out of it and survive long enough to take away the dreams of a girl who is so much better than you are.

"That innocent girl down there, whose parents you killed right in front of her, and for what? So the railroad could lay tracks through the middle of her dreams?"

Oliver's Colt barked again, shattering Spurlock's Derringer and the now useless left hand that had attempted to aim it at him.

Releasing the tails of his overcoat, Oliver closed and buttoned it, then picked up Spurlock's gun and walked over to the beautiful black mare. After removing her bridle and stuffing it into one of the saddle bags, he headed her back down the lane and said, "You can do better," before smacking her rump and sending her bolting into the darkening woods.

As the Washoe Kid lay writhing in pain and whimpering like a petulant child who had just had the definition of "manners" explained to him, he pleaded, "Please. Just kill me!"

"I'm not killing you," muttered Marshal Blackstone, dismissively stepping over Spurlock and walking into the trees to gather the firewood he'd collected earlier. Before heading back towards the house, he paused only briefly to say, "Charlie Spurlock, you are now an unarmed, non-threatening, pathetic piece of shit. That would be murder, and I'm not going to Hell... for you!"

Despite the hollow threats and obscenities shouted after him, Oliver ignored them. The center of his universe was down there at the bottom of that hill, peering anxiously out the door of what would soon be their home together.

Just like the Washoe Kid up there in the woods, whose screams were now intermingled with the unmistakable sound of ravenous wolves, Oliver Blackstone was leaving everything else behind him.

The next morning, a beautifully outfitted black mare showed up in Virginia City without its rider. The Washoe Kid never left that forest, nor was he ever heard from again.

The arrogance of the ignorant is forever their downfall. They convince themselves that they are invincible and that their actions, no matter the pain and suffering they cause to others, will never be visited upon them. However, karma is not exclusive to the human race. Good begets good, and the evil that men do will always find its way home to them.

Three years earlier, a young female wolf who'd been caught in a trapper's inhumane snare was at the brink of death, with little hope of survival. When Donovan Hampton discovered her, he not only showed mercy by releasing her, but he also showed her compassion by carrying her to the water that she, herself, could not reach, although her thirst was so great. When she was hungry but could not hunt, he shared his family's food with her. When her paw became infected, he cleaned and bandaged it for her, and allowed her to take shelter in his barn next to Mae until it healed. Donovan did all of these things without denying her the freedom to either accept or decline his generous gifts.

Later, when that wolf bore offspring of her own, Donovan welcomed them into his family's idyllic refuge, where they could hunt and rest and frolic and hone their skills without fear of persecution for being that which God had created them to be.

Six months ago, when Charlie Spurlock killed Donovan and Beverly Hampton, he had not only broken the heart of a frightened young girl, but he had also shattered that of a mother wolf, for she had loved them too.

CHAPTER 23

SARAH AND MIA were waiting expectantly at the doorway when Oliver came back over the hill towards the house. Upon seeing him, they both breathed audible sighs of relief and walked out onto the porch to meet him.

"Is everything all right, honey?" asked Sarah.

"We heard shooting up on the hill," added Mia.

"Everything is fine, my angels. In fact, it couldn't be better," said Oliver, kissing both of them despite the bundle of firewood in his arms.

"Who was shooting up there?" asked Mia, visibly worried that there had been some kind of trouble.

"I was the only one doing any kind of shooting, sweetheart," said Oliver. "While I was up on the ridge getting some firewood, I noticed a varmint had come a little bit too close to the house, so I just got rid of it before it could become a problem."

"Was it a rattlesnake? I'll bet it was a rattlesnake," Mia posited, while nodding to herself.

"You know, I'm pretty sure that's exactly what it was, now that I think about it," Oliver noted.

"Well then, I'm glad you got rid of it, because you can never trust a rattlesnake," Mia reminded him.

"Amen to that," said Oliver, as he stepped inside with the firewood, and Sarah closed the door behind them.

With the amount of construction underway due to the Comstock Lode, Virginia City and the surrounding areas were experiencing a boom in population, often making it difficult to acquire lumber and other building supplies. After Mia had given him her father's construction ledger, Oliver was anxious to return the property to the condition in which it had been prior to the fire and the flood, and had created a list of items for the project which were much more readily-available back east.

Since it was their final day and night in the house before they departed, Oliver suggested they all ride into town, giving Sarah and Mia another opportunity to visit with Auntie Karen while Oliver attended to procuring the items on his list.

"That would be delightful," said Sarah. "Besides, there are so many things for us to talk about, and this time, we won't be in a rush."

"And I want to hear more about Little Ollie Blackstone!" blurted Mia with a childish grin, cutting her eyes towards Oliver without actually looking at him.

"Why does that not surprise me?" Oliver replied, adding, "I'm sure I'll be hearing a lot about Little Ollie Blackstone myself, over the next few days during our trip to Boston."

When they arrived in Virginia City, it was already a glorious autumn day, and once they reached Karen's store, Oliver could have exploded into a cloud of fairy dust, and not one of them would have noticed. Within minutes, they were so engrossed in their conversations, they only vaguely noticed him leaving.

Despite him being the wallflower at this particular party, he was happy to have the beginnings of the family he'd dreamt of for so long. For him, Karen *was* his mother. Although he would always honor his biological mom, Abigail, for fighting like hell to make sure that she would live to bear her son, when she died, Oliver was far too young to remember her. What he remembered was the smell of the gun shop; Karen's and Jedediah's heartfelt laughter; and the certainty of knowing that when he decided to hang up his marshal's badge for good, there would always be family and a place that he could call home.

Ten minutes after delivering Sarah and Mia to the family archivist, he knocked politely and entered the office of Sheriff Walsh.

"Good morning, sheriff," Oliver said, extending his arm for a handshake, warmly received by Frederick Walsh.

"Right back at you," said the sheriff, adding, "I was just thinking about you an hour ago."

"And for what did I deserve such an honor?" asked Oliver, with an unrevealing smile.

"Well, take a seat, because you'll want to be sitting when you hear about it."

As Oliver sat down, the sheriff poured coffee for him into a mug, then took a seat behind his desk, leaning back and crossing his legs with the heels of his boots on the desktop.

"This morning, someone found a black mare, all decked out in a fancy black saddle and studded saddlebags. She'd been freshly shoed, and there was not a scratch on her, but she was riderless," the sheriff explained.

"That sounds a lot like the Washoe Kid's horse," noted Oliver, before asking, "Was there any sign of him?"

"Neither hide nor hair," answered the sheriff, adding, "But, I can't imagine that he'd have just stood by and watched someone ride off with her."

"Are you sure she didn't pull off of a hitching post somewhere?" Oliver asked.

"Most horses need a bridle to be tied to a hitching post," stated Sheriff Walsh.

"And she didn't have one?" queried Oliver.

"Oh, she had one all right, but it had been removed and neatly folded together, then stuffed into one of her saddlebags," said the sheriff. "Anyone possessing the gall to do that either has a death wish, or they knew damn well that he wouldn't be coming after them. I kind of feel like it's the latter," he added.

"And why might that be?" asked Oliver.

"Because that fancy pearl-handled peacekeeper of his was stuffed into the other saddlebag," Frederick chuckled. "He might let someone walk off with his horse, but to get his gun from him, someone would have had to take it, and that's not even the crazy thing," laughed the sheriff aloud.

"And, what's the crazy thing?" Oliver asked.

"The gun was as clean as a horny dog's balls, and all six rounds were still in the chamber. Whoever it was, took his horse and his gun from him, and he never got off a single shot. Not even one!" Sheriff Walsh explained, scratching his head.

"It sounds to me that either someone got tired of his shit and knocked him cold before he could slap leather, or there's a new player in town. Hell, he might even have been shanghaied and could already be on his way to China for all we know," suggested Oliver.

221

"China? Do you really think so?" asked the sheriff, as if seriously considering the possibility.

"Apparently, it happens more often than people think," said Oliver. "In fact, a few weeks ago, back in Boston, there was a big story in the Herald about it."

"A big story about what?" asked Deputy Pierce, walking in on the tail end of the conversation.

"People are getting shanghaied all over the place," said the sheriff. "Apparently, it's a trend big enough for even the Herald in Boston to report."

"What? Do you think that might be what happened to the Washoe Kid?" asked Jimmy, just as Deputy Haywood came through the door.

"What happened to the Washoe Kid?" asked Deputy Haywood, leaning back against the open door frame.

"The sheriff and the marshal here think he may have been shanghaied," said Deputy Pierce.

"So you think the Washoe Kid was shanghaied!" exclaimed Deputy Haywood, just as Jesse Bartlett was walking out of the hardware store next door, talking to the owner about how the Washoe Kid's horse had been aimlessly walking the streets earlier that morning.

"Hell, he could be on his way to China by now," said Deputy Haywood, somewhat louder than he probably should have.

"Goddammit!" shouted Jesse Bartlett, rushing down the dusty street on his skinny bowlegs. "They done shanghaied the Washoe Kid!"

The sheriff smiled and shook his head. "Deputies Pierce and Haywood, you two might want to go after him. We don't know for sure what happened to Spurlock, but we definitely don't need the town crier out there, panicking everyone in Virginia City... And close the damn door on your way out!" he shouted as the two deputies raced off after Jesse Bartlett.

Once they were alone again, Sheriff Walsh leaned in closer to Marshal Blackstone and said, in a somewhat lower tone, "Now, I'm just hypothesizing here, but what I really believe is that there is a new player in town, and that player is you."

Leaning back again, Sheriff Walsh said, "The last time you were here, I mentioned your name to Alfred, up at the International. I didn't ask him about you directly, so that he wouldn't have to lie to me, but when I mentioned your name, asking if he'd ever heard of you, his face went so ice-cold that I didn't recognize him anymore. He told me that if I didn't know who you were, then I definitely needed to do more homework, so I did," said the sheriff, sipping his coffee before continuing.

"Let's just say that you've done a lot of marshalling for such a young man, and judging by some of the names on your killed or captured felons list, there is only one person between here and the Mississippi River who could have possibly taken down the Washoe Kid. I thought there might be two, but I was wrong, and my ribs are a constant reminder of that miscalculation every day," said the sheriff, tenderly touching his side.

Oliver's smile revealed nothing as he continued to listen.

"I think he went out to your place and threatened you, Mia, and the Misses, and that you, while exercising your duties as a US marshal, gave him a second asshole between the eyes. Then, being the fine, upstanding marshal that you are, you put his weapon in one saddlebag, and the bridle in the other one, so the innocent little old mare out there wouldn't step on it or get it caught on something on her way back into town," concluded the sheriff, leaning back and placing his boots on the desktop again.

"That's an interesting story," said Oliver. After taking another sip of coffee, he added, "But I didn't kill Spurlock. If I had, I would have been required to report that, and then bring him into town on the back of his horse, and fill out all those pesky reports, only to end up with a reputation for being the man who killed the Washoe Kid on Mia's property."

Looking intensely into Walsh's eyes, he said, "That is Mia's home. She was born and raised there, and it's the only place where I have ever seen her truly happy. I'm not even allowed to kill a grasshopper on that property, because I promised her that I wouldn't. Can you imagine the heartache she would have felt if she had known the man who killed her parents had come there looking for her? It's the only place in the world where Mia can truly be Mia, and I am not the man to take that away from her.

"She may be a sophisticated young lady to the rest of the world, but to me, she will always be that frightened little child who needed a bag of licorice and a guardian angel, even if at first I was a reluctant one.

"For every name on the list you mentioned, there is a thousand dollars added to the outlaw bounty on my head. I refuse to be the lighthouse that draws the next hundred Washoe Kids to her front door. I couldn't do that. Not to my Mia. "

After a long pause, the sheriff pounded his fist on his desk and said, "Goddammit! They done shanghaied the Washoe Kid!"

CHAPTER 24

FOR SOME REASON Oliver believed that the train ride to Boston would be an editorial exposé on the life and times of "Little Ollie Blackstone." Obviously, he'd completely overlooked the seven-hour coach ride from Virginia City to Reno! After securing the house, they'd gotten underway promptly at 7:00 a.m., at which point Mia reminded everyone that they would reach Reno no later than 2:00 p.m., at least according to her infallible finger-clock.

By the time the first three of those fingers had ticked down, Oliver had been thoroughly refreshed on aspects of his childhood which he only barely remembered, while realizing they were things that Mia would never forget, nor allow *him* to again. Nevertheless, despite the hours-long "Do you remember when?" session, the Virginia City to Reno journey had never seemed shorter, or more entertaining to him.

As Sarah and Mia had occasionally immersed themselves in the dispatch received from Layla on the previous day regarding the wedding, Oliver reflected on the recent events that had brought them all together.

That working class restaurant where he'd eaten because his appearance had been far too unseemly to venture inside anyplace else, and how that delicious meal had become tasteless when the restaurant owner threatened to toss Mia out like dirty bathwater. That cringing feeling in his gut, which he had tried to ignore, when he knew those men in the restaurant had come to kill her, hours after she'd watched her parents die. Worst of all, in his mind, was how he'd hesitated and left her there because he didn't want to miss his train in Reno.

Although he had eventually come to his senses, his own personal shame of having nearly failed her was a deep-seated reminder that established maxims like, "It's never too late to do the right thing," are woefully inaccurate. Had he waited another ten minutes, it would have been too late, and his life right now would be vastly different and unimaginably emptier.

Her childish questions revealed the depth of her soul because, even in their apparent innocence, they challenged the wisdom behind his decisions, forcing him to face harsh realities that remained realities despite the discomfort he felt when confronted with them.

He'd spent five years living as a recluse, trying to accumulate the wealth that Sarah had been born into because her father told him he wasn't good enough, when, as Mia had forced him to acknowledge, he didn't want to marry her father anyway. He and Sarah had traded hundreds of dispatches, yet neither of them had been courageous enough to say the words that would have immediately given both of them the happiness they desired. They had themselves erected the barriers that separated them, and it had taken a seven-year-old girl to tear them down by forcing Oliver to add another four words to his dispatch. Of course, to be fair, she was almost eight.

When they reached Reno, it was, not surprisingly, almost exactly 2:00 p.m., and they proceeded directly to the Frontier Hotel.

"Mia!" shrieked Annie the moment the Blackstone trio came through the door, and she rushed across the lobby to meet the young lady holding a picnic basket containing a freshly laundered tablecloth and linen napkins, along with an empty mason jar that had also been meticulously cleaned.

Politely handing her the basket, Mia said, "Thank you for loaning this to us, Miss Annie."

"It was no bother at all," said Annie before yelling to the barkeeper, "Paul, would you mind helping them with their bags?"

"I'd be delighted to," answered Paul, smiling as he approached. "Welcome back, Marshal Blackstone, Mrs. Blackstone, and, of course, the ever delightful Mia Blackstone!"

"Thank you, Paul," said Oliver, shaking his hand and adding, "It's always a delight to stay here at the Frontier."

Paul quickly grabbed four of the six larger bags, and Oliver carried the other two, along with his own hardware. They were given the same rooms as on their previous stay, and after helping them get situated, the barkeeper was about to leave. Suddenly, he remembered something that had been on his mind for the entire week.

"Do you remember how you asked me why people called me Sam when my real name is Paul, and I told you how no one could seem to remember my real name?" he asked Mia.

"Yes," said Mia, smiling.

"Well, I was talking about that very thing with Annie, and she never knew my real name was Paul, so she just called me what everyone else called me. It was funny, because it made me think about it, and I realized that people only call me Sam, because I gave them that option. The very next day, I decided to stop doing that, and guess what?

"What?" asked Mia, her eyes wide with curiosity.

"Ever since that day, no one calls me Sam anymore. Everyone calls me Paul!" Shaking his head, he added, "It's the darndest thing."

Motioning frantically for him to come nearer, she cupped her hands around his ear and whispered, "That's because, as long as you keep them secret, birthday wishes can really come true." That was my birthday wish! Since it was for you, I guess it's okay that you know, but you can't tell anyone else, okay?"

Standing up straight again, Paul locked his lips with an imaginary key and smiled, saying, "It'll be our little secret," before handing her the "key" and heading back down the stairs.

Oliver and Sarah had no idea what she'd told Paul, but obviously it was a secret, so they didn't pry.

Later that afternoon, Oliver dropped Buddy and Kate off at the livery stable, assuring the owner, "I'll be back for them in two weeks, so don't go selling them again!"

"I wouldn't even dream of it," the man promised with a wink that left Oliver wondering if he'd actually stick to it or not.

As Oliver was leaving the stable, he was intercepted by a perplexed looking Deputy Marshal Cherry, who approached, saying, "Marshal Blackstone, do you have a minute?"

"Of course, what can I do for you?" Oliver replied, turning to face him.

"I just got a dispatch from Sheriff Walsh in Virginia City. He seems to think that Charlie Spurlock may have thrown in with the wrong crowd. They found his horse wandering along the road and believe it's possible he may have been shanghaied." Looking up suspiciously from beneath the brim of his hat, Deputy Cherry asked, "What do you make of that?"

"Well," said Oliver. "The way I see it, gone is gone, and whether he's in the belly of a slow-boat to China, or a pack of hungry coyotes, either way suits me just fine."

"I couldn't agree more," said the deputy, tipping his hat and adding, "Have a safe trip Marshal Blackstone."

Later that evening, following another enjoyable meal, Sarah and Oliver tucked Mia into her bed before retiring to their own room. They fell asleep as soon as their heads hit the pillows, some five hours later. Before that, those same heads hit the door of the room, the wall near the window overlooking the street, several areas on the polished wooden floor, and even the mirror on the ornate wooden dresser.

Each time Oliver's passion threatened to ebb, he would merely look at her. The vision of her lying there, clinging to him desperately and refusing to allow their union to be broken, refired his libido, pushing both him and Sarah up to and beyond the point of ecstasy, until at last they fell into an exhausted sleep.

For Mia and Oliver, it would be their third time crossing the continent aboard the Transcontinental Railroad. Without regard to that fact, the views parading past the window of their cabin never seemed to fade in their majesty. The panoramic beauty of the Western

Frontier was like a songbird whose call could not be ignored, and the farther they ventured east, the more desperate the longing for their quaint little hidden paradise became.

When one has carried the weight of the world upon their shoulders for so long, being freed from the task of carrying it alone is more than liberating; it's transformational.

As Oliver stood at the altar, dressed in a tuxedo fit for the Prince of Wales, that weight was lifted the very moment Mia emptied the final petals from her basket of roses, and Sarah appeared at the end of the aisle, wearing a wedding gown that would be the envy of Boston high-society for decades to come; a dress designed and hand-sewn by the ever-devoted Layla, the only candidate she had ever even considered to serve as her Maid of Honor.

When Leonard merged with Sarah and offered her his arm to escort her down the aisle of the Old North Church, even the midnight ride of Paul Revere could not compare to the midday walk of Sarah Blackstone in the heart of her exceedingly proud father.

Words and rings were exchanged again, and love, already so bright as to outshine the stars, shone even brighter when Sarah, Oliver, and Mia Blackstone, receded down that aisle as a family, and into the ages, together.

And did they all live happily ever after?

Of course they did. But this was not the end of their story.

EPILOGUE

SARAH, OLIVER, AND Mia arrived back in Reno, Nevada as scheduled, and spent another night there at the Frontier Hotel, with the many individuals who had been pivotal characters in their amazing journey.

As they crossed through seven hours of terrain between Reno and their home alongside Donovan Creek, the breathtaking two-hundred-seventy-degree view was no longer diminished by the ninety degrees reserved for the two enormous asses, Buddy, and Kate. The reliable, hard-working mules had been missed just as much as everything else attached to their enchanted little kingdom in the woods.

Oliver and Sarah were so at ease as they worked together to recreate Donovan's "Indian earring" wonderland. After rebuilding the laundry shed and bath houses with locally supplied products, Oliver went to work reconstructing the barn, which had actually straddled the creek, explaining why there were stone foundations on both banks. Inside the barn was a water wheel similar to those utilized on riverboats, and once completed, it powered nearly everything on the property.

There were no electric grids in 1874. However, once completed, the waterwheel inside the barn generated enough electricity to power simple light fixtures in each room of the house, the privy, the heated bath house, and the laundry shed, along with four additional light fixtures installed at each exterior corner to illuminate the porch that wrapped around their innovative log cabin in the woods.

Although Oliver was more familiar with firearms than with standard workman's tools, he found immense satisfaction in assembling the puzzles Donovan had left behind in generous supply. By Mia's ninth birthday, their home had both electricity and running water in every room; a fantastic achievement considering the rarity of such buildings in the mid- to late-1800s! It was also a timely one, because it made life much easier for Sarah and Mia's new baby brother, James Leonard Blackstone.

Although Mia was enthralled by her little brother, caring for him consumed an enormous amount of Sarah's time, often leaving Mia to her own devices. To remedy that imbalance, on her tenth birthday, Oliver and Sarah gifted her a puppy; a feisty little Jack Russell Terrier. Despite an exhaustive list of alternatives proposed by Oliver, Mia insisted on naming him

Little Ollie Blackstone, using it in its entirety each time she called out for him... which was constantly!

When Little Ollie Blackstone was seven months old, he began testing his limits. Although he wasn't supposed to leave the yard or the grassy hillside across from it, one morning, while playing with Mia, he took off into the woods. Little Ollie Blackstone refused to come back when she shouted out to him, "Little Ollie Blackstone! Little Ollie Blackstone!" for approximately half an hour until he was summarily chastened and escorted back to the yard by Mama Wolf. To no one's surprise, that was a stunt he never attempted again.

During the day, Sarah continued the extraordinary education of Mia during her brother's afternoon naps. Her thirst for knowledge was unquenchable, and Sarah was fascinated by the level of attention she dedicated to each and every lesson. She was only eleven years old when she presented Sarah with the most astounding gift she'd ever received: a clearly legible, wonderfully written, and colorfully illustrated book she had created especially for Sarah, entitled *Little Ollie Blackstone and Me.*

Mia Blackstone would continue her journey as an author, creating dozens more such children's books, all of which Sarah would dutifully read and edit for Mia before submitting the manuscripts for copyright protection.

One such book was entitled *The Silver War*, and just as she was about to correct what she thought was an error in the title, she thought better of it and opened the book to begin reading it instead.

Mia had opened the chest.

The book was inspired by the lives of her biological parents, Donovan and Beverly Hampton, whose stories began in Kentucky. Theirs was a love story for the ages, and despite the obstacles they faced while first working their way north during the Civil War, only to be rejected by his father, Alexander Hampton, who loved his own prestige more than he loved his academically brilliant son.

After refusing to submit to Alexander's demands, Donovan and Beverly joined a wagon train headed west, in search of greener pastures, silver, and gold on the Western Frontier. With a life savings of only three hundred dollars, Donovan bought ten acres of land along an overgrown stream, and while clearing it, he discovered gold in the glimmering waters of what would become known as Donovan Creek.

Realizing the potential risk they would face had their discovery been revealed, Donovan collected and hid it from everyone beyond the tree line of the property they'd purchased.

Soon, he had nearly fifty thousand dollars' worth of gold and began using it to realize his engineering potential, eventually building and patenting over a hundred different unique inventions.

Reading on, Sarah was amazed to find that Beverly had never even gone to Virginia City, nor had she ever wanted to. The paradise Donovan had built for them was the most peaceful place on Earth for her, and when Mia was conceived, her happiness was complete.

Donovan continued to build and create, and by the time he'd finished his innovative self-panning system, they were so wealthy, they didn't even need the gold anymore. What he needed was the power of the flowing water to build and test his inventions and continue his lifelong journey of discovery.

The final entry to his private journal was on the night of the fire, before leaving with Beverly and Mia, in an attempt to reach the sheriff in Virginia City, a good man named Frederick Walsh.

The entry read, *"I am attempting to flee with my darlings Beverly and Mia to Sheriff Walsh in Virginia City. Beverly and I will never submit to the vile hatred we've crossed a continent to escape, and Sheriff Walsh is a good man who I know in my heart I can trust. My own life is of little value if I cannot save my precious wife and children, both born and unborn, and if it is my life I must give to save them, then give it I shall. Donovan Lee Hampton, signed this 27th day of March, in the year of our Lord, 1872."*

Sarah was crushed, but so many things now made sense to her. Donovan had built this particular paradise specifically so that his children could grow up free of the biases that lay beyond the magical hills surrounding them. Donovan Creek was an island from the noise, where he could create things for the betterment of all mankind, believing, as he'd written in another journal entry, that *"The earth is full of miracles, yet we wage war over the most mundane of things. If abundance can belong to everyone, then no man, woman, or child need ever know a deficit."*

This was the passion that fueled the brilliant Donovan Hampton. His only wish was to leave an enduring legacy for his daughter, Mia, and the sibling she would now never have an opportunity to meet, to know, and above all, to love.

Mia's manuscript, *The Silver War*, included two documents of the utmost importance to her. The first was a completed bill of sale, and the other was a photograph of the property Donovan had purchased: Mia's mother, Beverly.

The documents were as much an admonition to society as they were a declaration of true love from Donovan

Hampton. Finding no other place where the love of his wife, Beverly, would be wholeheartedly embraced, he'd decided to build one... just for her.

Although Mia had heard the words of hate chanted outside their house that night, when the "bad men" burned down their barn, she was far too young to comprehend them, when all she could think of was her beloved milk cow, Mae.

Sheriff Walsh had tried to help by taking Mia to a successful Black business owner, a woman named Nancy, who ran the restaurant where Oliver had first encountered her. However, since Mia's features were decidedly more Anglo Saxon than Negro, she was deemed akin to dirty bathwater, a cutting, derogatory term used to describe Mulatto children, in a moment when that should not have even mattered.

The title of Mia's book wasn't an error at all. It perfectly captured the reality of being forced into a deadly conflict with one's own friends, neighbors, and family members, or looking to the west with the hopes of a better future, made possible by the Comstock Lode. Those were the only options for Donovan and Beverly Hampton: silver, or war.

After finishing Mia's manuscript, Sarah set it aside and walked out onto the porch overlooking their little corner of paradise. Oliver was pushing Leonard on the swing, attached to the oak tree that Donovan had imported from Kentucky, as a reminder that even things born in the south can thrive in the west.

They never built on the property Oliver purchased in Springfield, Massachusetts. Instead, he gifted it to Mia's mentor and Sarah's sister, Layla Reese, when they returned to Boston one final time to attend the funeral of Leonard Hutchins. Once the estate was settled, Sarah donated the Hutchins compound in its totality, which was then converted to a school for gifted children, and later into a historical landmark near the Old North Church.

After having seen the photo of Beverly, it was obvious to Sarah and Oliver why Mia had taken to Layla so quickly. She and Beverly could have been twins, and during the six months in which Mia had been under Layla's daily supervision, she'd acquired those same qualities of charm, grace, and sincerity that Layla had also instilled in Sarah, and which Oliver found so endearing in both of them.

Marshal Oliver Blackstone never officially retired from the US Marshals Service, but he never again raised his Colt at another man. However, he did teach little James Leonard Blackstone how to use one, and at thirty paces, he could strike a match with it!

Overall, the Blackstone family was blessed with many gifts, the greatest of which was their love for one another. Even so, although Sarah knew there could never be a love greater than the one she and Oliver shared, there had always been, and would always be, a special connection and an unbreakable bond that would endure throughout the ages: the bond between Oliver and Mia.

"Little Ollie Blackstone, Little Ollie Blackstone! Get over here! Right now!"

THE END

A Message from The Author

While authoring this book, I was often torn by my ever-present desire to provide the historically accurate context upon which I build my novels. At a time when our nation was torn apart, and people were forced to choose country over family, not everyone fell victim to the mentality of either/or. Some chose to search for a different alternative, and that alternative was most likely to be found west of the Mississippi River.

Despite that fact, as people moved to Virginia City, Nevada in search of silver and gold, they often brought their fears, biases, and misplaced anger with them. All too often, those attributes escalated into conflicts which led to murder, death, and mayhem, albeit on a smaller scale than the American Civil War raging in other parts of the country.

After much consideration, I simply decided to tell a story of an enchanting young girl, an upstanding morally guided man, and the opportunity to choose love over anger, peace over division, and humanity over cruelty. Their physical descriptions are intentionally left open to interpretation, allowing everyone to enjoy the amazing tale of love and good prevailing over evil, for good and evil have no faces. They are actions taken with intent, as I truly believe that both good and evil, like so many other things that affect our daily lives, are choices. Unfortunately, people often go to great lengths while attempting to justify the evil actions that benefit them, while so often failing to comprehend that honorable deeds do not require further justification.

The story of Oliver and Mia is about two people who have every right to doubt humanity, but instead choose to spread a love that shines so brightly that it beautifully blinds us to everything else.

With two such powerful leading personalities, it was essential for me to introduce you to the content of their characters and the respectful manner in which they treat others, rather than to the physical attributes that are all too often an unconquerable obstacle that we, ourselves, erect.

In the end, I wanted Oliver to be Oliver and Mia to be Mia, in the eyes of their beholders, and if nothing else, I hope the story of Oliver and Mia has accomplished that objective.

Thank you for your readership!

Riano D. McFarland

Riano D. McFarland – Author

Riano McFarland is an American author and professional entertainer from Las Vegas, Nevada, with an international history.

Born in Germany in 1963, he is both the son of a retired US Air Force veteran and an Air Force veteran himself. After spending 17 years in Europe and achieving notoriety as an international recording artist, he moved to Las Vegas, Nevada in 1999, where he quickly established himself as a successful entertainer. Having literally thousands of successful performances under his belt, Riano is a natural when it comes to dealing with and communicating his message to audiences. His sincere smile and easygoing nature quickly put acquaintances at ease with him, allowing him to connect with them on a much deeper personal level—something that contributes substantially to his emotionally riveting style of storytelling. Furthermore, having lived in or visited many of the areas described in his novels, he can connect the readers to those places using factual descriptions and impressions, having personally observed them.

Riano has been writing poetry, essays, short stories, tradeshow editorials, and talent information descriptions for over 40 years, collectively. His style stands apart from many other authors in that, while his talent for weaving clues into the very fabric of his stories gives them depth and a sense of credulity, each of his novels is distinctly different from the others. Whether describing the relationship between a loyal dog and his loving owner in **ODIN**, following the development of an introverted boy-genius in **JAKE'S DRAGON**, chronicling the effects of extraterrestrial intelligence on the development and fate of all mankind in **THE ARTIFACT**, or describing the parallels between people and the objects they hold sacred in **I FIX BROKEN THINGS**, Riano tactfully draws you into an inescapable web of emotional involvement with each additional chapter and each new character introduced. Added to that, his painstaking research when developing plots and storylines gives his novels substance, which can hold up under even the staunchest of reader scrutiny.

Riano has an uncanny ability to build creative tension and suspense within a realistic plot. The result is that he draws readers into the story as if they were always meant to have a starring role in it. Furthermore, by skillfully blending historical fact with elements of fiction, Riano makes the impossible appear plausible, while his intensely detailed descriptions bring characters and locations vividly into focus.

Although it's certain you'll love the destination to which he'll deliver you, you'll never guess the routes he'll take to get you there, so you may as well just dive in and enjoy the ride, which is certain to keep you on the edge of your seat until the very last paragraph!

Made in United States
Orlando, FL
30 January 2023